I0631017

Deep inside the huge space ship, the Oligarch spoke to three chosen starmen. "It would be dangerous to try to work secretly. If they were to discover us in the midst of planting the explosive, it would be fatal. We'll go down and ask the Earthmen their permission. You will learn their language and when we land, lull their natural suspicions. It will be your responsibility to see that we blow up the planet on schedule!

"I don't need to tell you that you can't fail."

THE FLAME OF IRIDAR
Lin Carter

TWO COMPLETE, FULL LENGTH SCIENCE FICTION NOVELS

PERIL OF THE STARMEN
Kris Neville

WILDSIDE PRESS

FLAME OF IRIDAR/PERIL OF THE STARMEN

CONTENTS

DEDICATION

The Flame of Iridar

This book is for

EDMOND HAMILTON AND
LEIGH BRACKETT

A minima ad maximis

Flame of Iridar

PROLOGUE

Dimly red against the evening sky, Mars hangs like a great jewel gone dead and lusterless with age. Across her endless miles of crimson desert, a thin and bitter wind whispers . . . driving dry sand over the broken walls of her dead cities, that brood forever over the powdered bones of her vanished Kings . . .

But ten million years ago, when Earth was ruled by monster reptiles and the first men were naked animals huddling together in jungle depths, Mars was a living world. Under clear skies, where two moons lit the dark, great oceans drove . . . waves battered against the cliff-built citadels of young, barbaric nations, where Wizards, Gods and Kings struggled to carve out empires with notched and dripping swords, and fearless men wrote bloody pages in histories our own scientists will soon puzzle over, striving to decipher from their cryptic glyphs the mighty tales and sagas of the Dawn Age of Mars.

This is one of them.

1 TWILIGHT IN SHIANGKOR

THE DRAGON banner of Shiangkor caught the freshening
evening breeze and unfolded in writhing coils of scarlet
and green, above the towered height where the King stood.
But he had eyes only for the small, battered figure far
below on the long stone quay, where the *Seriphosa* rode at
anchor with yellow sails furled, discharging her precious
cargo of one lonely man.

King Niamnon watched as the youth was brought ashore,
bound and shackled, and as he watched his strong hands
clutched the window bars so tightly that his flashing rings
bit into the flesh.

"At last," he hissed softly. "The last drop of Guthrum's
blood! And with his death, the House of Orm is extin-
guished!"

"A slow death, Lord King? And an ingenious one?"

The King turned. Behind him stood the eldest of his
royal councilors, the Enchanter, Sarkond.

"Slow or fast—what matters is that he dies, and another
Kingdom is added to my empire. But I have no belly for
these lingering deaths you so skillfully draw out, Enchanter.
He is a strong man, Chandar, and for all that I hate his
blood, I have no wish to see him reduced to the level of a
groveling animal by your . . . *artistry.*"

The last word was spat in contempt, but the lean Enchanter only smiled and bowed slightly. Niamnon turned
back to the window to watch the heavily guarded procession
make its slow, winding way up the steep and cobbled street
toward the Hall.

They were strangely unlike . . . and yet alike . . . the
King and his advisor. Tall and manly of build, Niamnon
of Shiangkor was in his fortieth year, but only threads of

9

grey shot the bristling black beard and close-cropped skull
that bore the Winged Golden Dragon in place of a crown.
The iron thews of his conquering youth drew tight the
scarlet silk of his tunic, and when the chill sea wind blew
wide his fur-trimmed royal cloak, the massive breadth of
his shoulders bore plain witness to his legendary strength.
But something in his eyes, a coldness, an icy fury . . .
and something in the cruel, sneering twist to his thin lips
. . . gave witness, too, that here was a man driven almost
to madness by the unholy lust for power.

By contrast, the Enchanter was a slim, lean man whose
age could be read only in his slitted emerald eyes. His
smooth, saffron skin was drawn tight over the hairless skull
and gaunt cheeks, unmarred by wrinkles. But *age* . . .
corrupt centuries . . . burned like guttering candles of
corpse fat in the inhuman lustre of his eyes. He was
wrapped from throat to heel in a long gown of dull green,
clasped at the narrow waist by a girdle of linked copper
discs, from which strange implements hung by little chains.
Talismans and sigils . . . the tools of the Black Art. And
in his lean, motionless form one sensed the same greed for
empery . . . for power over men's bodies, minds and . . .
souls?

The Enchanter spoke again, a soft whispering voice.

"He has worked much mischief against Shiangkor, Lord
King. I only spoke to suggest a fitting . . . punishment
. . . for the years he has inconvenienced your imperial
plans."

The King turned impatiently from the window.

"Enough—snake of a man! He shall die, be assured of
that. He has slipped through our fingers a dozen times, but
now we have him fast. Bother me no more with your tor-
tures—go, summon the court. We shall sit in triumph over
this Chandar of Orm!"

The Enchanter bowed again, a cold smile flitting across
his thin lips.

"I shall fulfill your orders, Lord King. In this, as in all
things, Sarkond is your loyal servant."

Chandar of Orm planted his booted feet wide and stared
up insolently into the face of King Niamnon. His leather

tunic, its tattered rags now little more than a loin-cloth, bared a powerful sun-bronzed body as strongly thewed as the King's own, but lithe and supple with the agility of youth. From head to foot he was covered with scarlet ribbons of blood which had clotted into dry brown flakes where his wrists were tightly bound behind his back. He looked every inch the bold corsair, whose wit and heroic daring had held off the mighty fleets of Shiangkor for three years.

He spoke no word, made no obeisance, but met the King's burning gaze as coolly as an equal.

Niamnon, gorgeous in jeweled robes, leaned back on the great ivory throne carven from a single tusk of a great sea dragon, and looked the youth over in silence. The boy (for he was scarcely more than that) surely bore the blood of Guthrum of Orm: it showed in his unruly mane of ink black hair that poured in blood-matted tangle down his brawny shoulders . . . in the fearless gaze of his ice-blue eyes, startlingly pale in the leather-bronzed face . . . and in the unyielding set of his strong, clean-shaven jaw.

"How was he taken?" the King spoke at last. A scar-faced seaman stepped forward, saluting with the flat of his blade over his heart.

"Off the Bay of Nephelis, Lord King. His ship, the *Ormsgard,* was dimasted in a storm the night before. Admiral Kralian's squadron had been in pursuit for three days with never a sign of the pirate scum, until we came upon the hulk wallowing in a welter of wreckage."

"Why is our Admiral not here?"

"Wounded, Lord King."

"Badly?"

The seaman shrugged. "The surgeons say he will lose his right arm, Lord King, but that he will live. The corsairs had fought the storm for a day and a night without sleep, but they fought us like demons from hell!"

"Where are the other prisoners?"

The seaman laughed—then checked himself, remembering the royal presence. "Food for the merfolk, Lord King! They fought to the death—even after we struck down their leader, here. He and—that one there," he nodded at a giant bull of a man, hung with chains enough to bind

a savage *kreagar,* who stood behind the youth, growling
and swearing in the thickness of an immense red beard.
"After Chandar fell to a sword blow—the flat of a blade
across the temple—that bush-bearded bull fought over
him until the sword broke off in his hand. It took nine men
to bind him."

Niamnon dismissed the seaman with a curt nod, rose
slowly from the ivory throne, and descended the seven steps
of the dais slowly, to stand in front of the bound youth
who still had not spoken.

"Well, wolf-whelp?" the King grated. "What shall we
do with you, eh?"

Sarkond emerged from the silent throng of gaily-clad
courtiers, stepping forward on whispering sandals.

"Be careful, Lord King. Even bound, he is dangerous."

"I fear no man alive," Niamnon snorted. "Well, whelp
of Orm? How shall I repay you for the years you and your
corsair fleets hounded my ports?" He leaned forward, his
face only inches from the silent captive's.

"Shall I cut off your right arm—eh? As you did Kralian's
—and make you eat it, morsel by morsel? Eh? Answer me,
you base-born pup!" With a backhanded blow, he slashed
the boy across the cheek with his mace of office, its jewels
raking red furrows in the sun-browned flesh.

Chandar took no notice of the blow. He spoke at last,
in calm and measured tones.

"A clean death is too much to expect from you. Do with
me what you will."

The throng stirred and tittered. The King relaxed, grinning.

"It is a pity you are not wed, whelp! Then we could give
you the sort of death we gave your father. Do you remember? You were a skinny, pale-faced runt then. Do you
remember how we tied your mother down to watch, and
burnt your father alive—slowly?"

Chandar spat in the King's taunting face.

The room went silent, deathly still. No one dared to
speak or move in all the great hall save for the burly red-
bearded giant, who roared with laughter.

"That's it, lad! He's slime himself, the King of Dogs—
a little more slime won't harm!"

White to the lips, the King straightened, drawing a
jeweled hand over his mouth, wiping away the spittle
slowly.

"You shall die . . . like an animal," he said at last.
"You shall die like an animal, screaming for mercy."

Chandar smiled.

"I hope that I shall die like a man. My royal father,
men say, never cried out. Try me."

The King ascended the dais again.

"Tomorrow Chandar of Orm dies in the arena," he said
in slow, ringing words. "So that all may see, I declare public
festival. We shall pit him—unarmed—against the caged
monsters our gamekeepers have brought from the Southlands. We shall see this bravery in action! And now, take
this whelp and his companion to the dungeons, and guard
him well. Tomorrow, the sands of the arena shall be scarlet with the last blood of the House of Orm!"

Trumpets rang, a brazen peal that echoed among the
mighty beamed rafters, as the King withdrew and the two
pirates were taken away.

And Sarkond the Enchanter smiled, mirthlessly.

2 GREEN MAGIC

THE SLIMY stone wall was rough and cold against his naked
back. The cell was pitch-black, but after some hours his
eyes became enough accustomed to the dark to make out
shapes dimly, by a feeble ray that penetrated the massive
pile of masonry above him.

They had chained him with arms spread to the wall,
so that he could neither sit or recline, and with time the
ache of strained muscles became a dull red mist of pain
that receded into the background of his consciousness, lost
amid the throbbing of his untended wounds and the dank,
biting chill of the dungeon's foul-smelling, icy air.

Bound to the opposite wall, red-bearded Bram slum-

bered deeply, as if drugged. Chandar wished he could sleep
. . . so as to gather every bit of his strength for the trials
of tomorrow . . .

Tomorrow . . .

Chandar shrugged, wincing at the pain in his weary
shoulders. A few more hours of darkness, and then the
blinding morning sun on the arena sands . . . a few moments of scarlet pain . . . and he would rest . . . forever.

Was this the end, then? It was, surely. Only a miracle
of the Gods could save him now. The Gods! His lips
twisted, wryly. He had lost faith in the Gods that never-
forgotten night when the iron legions of Shiangkor brought
fire and sword into the great hall of Ormsgard . . . that
night when he was twelve, and the world ended . . .

He remembered it all. The black fleets of Shiangkor
stealing into the midnight fjord . . . the grim, mailed soldiers . . . swords flashing in the torch-light, blood bright
on the oaken tables. In his mind's eye, Chandar saw it all
again . . . his tall brothers hacked down, his fair yellow-
haired sister, Alixia, pinned to the wall with a spear . . .
his father, King Guthrum, roaring, leaping over the table,
seizing the famous and ancient Axe of Orm from the
wall . . .

And he remembered his kill, the notch-eared grinning
soldier who felled his brother, Arn, with a slashing, disem-
boweling stroke. He remembered himself, a scared boy,
springing to the soldier's back with a knife in his teeth,
the knife that cut open a throat and tasted blood for the
first time . . .

All his world was gone. His father, standing bound to
the kingpost of Ormsgard Hall, standing tall and proud and
silent as the flames licked at his legs, his hips, his chest
. . . while his mother, a moaning, blood-spattered thing,
died on the floor and the walls of the keep came crashing
down. All were dead, his family, his House, his Kingdom
. . . only he escaped, he and Bram the burly guard captain
who tossed him over his shoulder and bore him off in the
night, away from the blazing ruin . . . down to the sea.

Yes, the sea was both father and mother to him, in the
years that followed. He and Bram had found haven among
the corsairs of the Hundred Isles, where Bram's bull-strong

thews and Chandar's pitiful story had won admiration and
respect from the pirates. There they took oath and joined
the Brotherhood of the Free-Rovers . . . years of fresh
sea air and burning sun, hard work and good comradeship
among exiles and freebooters . . . years of harrying the
seacoast cities of Shiangkor, and bringing ruin to the mer-
cantile fleets of the growing little empire that had swallowed his homeland, as it had a dozen other realmlets.

Years of revenge! Yes, he had tasted the sweet wine of
hot revenge to the full. For with the iron strength of Bram
beside him, and driven by his bitter desire to avenge himself and his House, he had accomplished feats of daring that
wrung many a delighted oath from sea rovers thrice his
age. He was the first to swing over the gunwales of a Shiangkori ship . . . the last to leave her blood-bathed decks.
It had been his daring plot to creep by night in dark ships
with muffled oars into Delphontis harbor, and beard Niamnon's fat Governor in his palace, carrying off enough loot to
buy a Kingdom.

Aye, he had risen among the pirates, risen to be their
Prince, when grizzled old Dregorth fell. They had hailed
him then, his bold comrades, hailed him *Prince of Pirates*
while the twin moons stared down and the red wine ran
wet and free . . .

Then years of systematic sea war. Twice the navy of
Shiangkor had come limping back, unsuccessful from an
attempt to win another Kingdom by stealth and treachery,
as they had once won Orm. Proud Orcys in the north countries he had saved, Orcys whose pink marble spires rose
slim and cool beside the Dashpar, where it rushed to join
Jalangir Val, the Great Sea. And Nemour in the south, the
ancient friend of the Orm Kings, her wooded hills and
deep fjords were free, too, of the iron hand of Shiangkor.
Each time his agents had spied the fleets of Niamnor in
time for the corsair navy to muster and meet the hosts that
sought to steal empire . . . but earned death.

For three full years of open warfare, the corsair prince
of the Hundred Isles held the angry fleets of Shiangkor at
bay, darting forth to sink a merchantman or sack a coastal
town—then darting back to safety, to their unknown port
deep in the uncharted labyrinth of the Hundred Isles! Chan-

dar grinned at the memory. His red galley, the *Ormsgard,*
had been the fastest thing afloat in the Great Sea . . .
manned with a crew of picked fighters who swore by the
name of Chandar of Orm . . . and then he sobered. Where
were they now?

Where was gallant, laughing Evarne of Psamathis, the
exiled scion of the Heptad, who could sing like an angel
. . . and fight like hell's fiercest devil? Where was wise
Ganelon, the shrewd ex-fisherman who had taught Chandar
all the lore of the sea and her mysterious ways? And where
was stout Arik, as fearless as a red-maned *thanth?* Arik,
who had saved him that time off Illionar when the archer
put an arrow through his arm, and had another ready for
his heart—till stopped by a thrown sword.

Where? He laughed harshly—they were where he would
be by this time tomorrow. Dead. And perhaps, in the Land
of Shadows they would all meet again, beyond the Gates
of Life and Death . . .

What was that?

Chandar stiffened, and strained his ears. Nothing . . .
nothing, but the endless drip—drip—drip of icy water from
the roof beams, and the occasional scurry and rustle of a
rat . . .

There it was again—

"Chandar."

The faintest whisper of sound, but his ears caught it. He
turned his head from side to side—

Against the dark, a green spark burned.

Burned and grew . . . becoming a dim haze of green
light . . . growing stronger, catching glints of dim green
fire from pools of stagnant water and dull iron chains.
Painting a dim green man-form against the darkness.

Magic.

The glow strengthened, pulsed, and—died. Where it
had been, a tall, gaunt figure stood, wrapped from throat
to heel in a dull green robe . . . the Enchanter . . .

The Enchanter smiled, mockingly.

"How do you find the Lord King's hospitality, Prince
of Orm? Is it to your liking?" He gestured with one hand,
touching a sigil that dangled from his girdle of small plates,
and a sourceless glow lit the cell. Chandar glanced at Bram,

who slept on, and then a reckless spirit of merriment filled him.

"As gracious as your manners, dog of wizardry! Is it typical of Shiangkori politeness, to enter a King's bed-chamber without announcement? Or did you come to bring me a warm posset, to sooth my slumbers?" His voice rang clear and light in the weird yellow light.

Again the gaunt Enchanter smiled.

"You have spirit, Prince of Orm; I am glad they have not wrung that from you. I am Sarkond of K'thom, and I am no enemy of you or your unfortunate House. Indeed, I am your friend . . . I must in honesty add: your only friend in this peril."

"If you are my friend, Enchanter, then prove it by striking off these chains and putting a sword in my hands," Chandar laughed.

Iron rang against wet cobbles, and the youth sagged against the wall, weary arm-muscles slack. The chains lay at his feet! He slowly raised his arms before his face, and painfully flexed his cramped fingers, glancing at the smiling Enchanter.

"What—"

"I have struck the chains from you. You are free, Chandar of Orm. Now, am I not your friend?"

Tightening his jaw against the ache of stretching muscles, Chandar stood away from the dungeon wall, rubbing tingling life back into his naked muscles.

"Is this a trick? A little torture—make me think I'm free, then call in a dozen guards? Is that it?" he demanded.

"Listen to me, Prince of Orm. I am in deadly earnest. I came here tonight to set you free, and to take you far from this place. If you agree to my proposal, with the morning you will be on a ship and a free man . . . with a chance to strike a mighty blow against this madman of a King who calls me "snake"—free to win back your Kingdom, if that is your wish!"

Chandar regarded him, thoughtfully. All his instincts told him Sarkond was as trustworthy—and as friendly—as the winged vipers of the jungle lands. But . . .

"Say on, wizard. I shall mock you no more."

"Then listen, and listen well. Time is short. I am minister of Shiangkor and know that Niamnor will not be satisfied with Orcys and with Nemour, anymore than he was when he took Delphontis and Orm. He wants the world. I am privy to all his secrets, and I know what is next. First those two kingdoms to north and south, which you and your corsairs kept him from taking. Then a war with the Heptad is in his plans . . . his fleets will round the Delphontine penninsula and gain entrance into the Inner Sea and thence to Heptopolis itself."

"He will find Lord Spherian no easy man to whelm," Chandar interrupted. The Enchanter shrugged.

"The Seven Cities cannot oppose him, they are too divided and quarreling among themselves, and Spherian . . . well, the Heptarch is an old man now, and the fires of his youth burn low . . . a slight decoction in his wine, perhaps, will help to dampen them."

Chandar tensed his jaw grimly.

"Venom, eh? Woman's work—or wizard's!"

"Perhaps. But if you join me and do a service from your great need—a service that will cost you naught—I will give you the details of his plans, the times and places at which he plans to strike. Yes, and I will transport you to the Hundred Isles where you can gather together the remnants of your broken corsairs, and lead them against him as before."

"At what price?"

"All I ask—"

Sarkond fell silent. Another spot of green lambent flame now hovered in mid-air . . . spreading and growing before their eyes . . . a pulsing shadow of green magic fire that formed itself slowly into a human form.

"More magic, wizard? Or does Niamnon know your arts as well?" Chandar demanded, stooping to seize up a length of chain.

Sarkond silenced him with a lifted hand.

"A servant of mine, and not one that you should fear . . ." His cold green eyes ran mockingly, appraisingly, over the almost naked body of the youth. "Unless you are less the man than you look!"

Before Chandar could reply, the pulsing shadow of light coalesced into . . . a woman.

She was lithe and slim, with flesh of smooth dark gold,
where Sarkond's skin was withered saffron. But a daughter
of K'thom to her last drop of blood. She had the supple,
boneless grace that made the dancers of K'thom prizes for
an Emperor's harem. Her long-lashed, tilted eyes were a
strange liquid green, flashing with mocking lights. Her
mouth, full, scarlet, delicious, laughed at Chandar as his
dazed eyes drank deep of her exotic beauty.

Her foaming mane of red-gold hair poured in glittering
cascades down slim, bare shoulders, falling to her narrow
waist. High, proud breasts were cupped in hammered silver,
and silver bangles tinkled at her graceful wrists and bare
ankles.

Chains of tiny silver bells were woven through her blazing mane. They made thin, chiming music when she moved.

Sarkond ignored Chandar's gaping amazement.

"A servant of mine, Mnadis," he said. "Girl, what
news?"

Without taking her jeweled green eyes from Chandar's,
she said: "All is in readiness, Magister! The King sleeps,
like a drowned hog after hours of carousal. The plans are
all accomplished."

"Awaiting only your agreement, Prince of Orm," the
Enchanter said, turning back to the youth.

"Agreement to what? You have not yet revealed the
price of your friendship," Chandar said.

"Say rather the price of your freedom . . . and your
revenge. All I ask is that you accept this gift—"

From beneath his dull green cloak, the gaunt sorcerer
withdrew a battered, scarred old axe. The sourceless yellow light drew a line of fire from its notched, razor edge,
revealing the Hawk graven upon the haft.

"The Axe!" Chandar exclaimed. The Enchanter handed
it to him and he hefted it, feeling a rush of blood beat
strongly within him. His father's weapon . . . the sacred
symbol of their blood . . . the Axe of Orm, that of old
had been borne in many battles by Gondomyr the Victorious, the legendary founder of his House. The Axe whose
fame rang down the generations to this day, in saga and
minstrel tale! Just to touch the worn bone handle was to
recover a fragment of his lost heritage.

"I stole it from Niamnon's treasure crypt," the Enchanter said, imperturbably.

Chandar blinked back sudden tears. "Say on, Enchanter! This gift buys much patience from me."

Sarkond withdrew a phial of black, inky fluid from his girdle, and handed it to the Prince of Orm.

"This potion is called the Sleeping Death. Drink it down and you will fall into a slumber so deep that to all eyes you will seem as one dead. In ten hours you will revive, as from a sound, refreshing sleep."

Chandar frowned, examining the crystal flask. "To what purpose?"

Mnadis strolled forward, hands on curved hips. "To save your life, corsair! Tomorrow morn, when the King's guards come to drag you to death, you will be—to all apparent signs—one who has already passed the grim Gates. Niamnon will have you then buried, and we shall disinter you and bear you off to a waiting ship."

"A skillful scheme," Chandar said grudgingly, "But what if he wreaks his frustrated revenge upon my—ah— 'corpse'? Can your magic arts bring life back to a hacked collection of severed limbs?"

Sarkond smiled thinly. "Corpses are sacred in this land— untouchable—sacrosanct to Drega, Goddess of the Dead. The King is a superstitious man . . . and I will accompany him to your cell, to interject a warning word, should he indeed go berserk with fury and attempt you harm."

"A warning word, eh? Better make it a pageful . . . I have no wish to wake up the shorter by a head!"

"Fear not. I am your friend."

Chandar glanced at him curiously. Was it possible this yellow snake of K'thom really was a friend? His instincts warned him to distrust the wizard's words . . . but . . . he *was* free . . . and he bore the Axe!

"What of the Axe? Will not the King's suspicions be aroused to find it by my body?"

"Again I say, fear not. I have thought of everything. I shall give you to drink of the phial, then cause by magic your chains to bind you to the wall again . . . and take back the Axe for safe-keeping. Within ten hours you will awake aboard my ship—at sea—unharmed."

Chandar regarded the still sleeping form of his red-bearded companion. "What of Bram?"

Sarkond shrugged eloquently. "The King must have something to exhibit in the arena. I have need only of you."

"I will not go without him."

The Enchanter's eyes blazed suddenly.

"You will either do as I say, and go free, c⁻ die with him tomorrow on the sands, beneath a *thanth*!"

Chandar laughed, ringingly.

"You are a fool, Enchanter! For all your sorcerous wisdom, you do not understand men. Bram has fought by my side a hundred times—aye, and saved my life more than once! I shall not be afraid to fight beside him one last time . . . and rather than sneak off by your magic drug and leave him to face death alone, I would spit in the jaws of a thousand *thanthi*."

Sarkond's face went livid, and a snarled curse twisted his skull-gaunt face into a mask of rage.

"You filth of Orm, you dare speak thus to me? Know you not that I can blast you where you stand?"

"With this in my hands," Chandar tossed the great Axe up and caught it as it fell, "I dare anything. Blast away—and blast your own secret purposes with me, whatever they are!"

"I'll—" began the wizard, but Mnadis laid a restraining hand upon his arm, and he fell silent.

She slid forward, facing the stubborn youth with the full force of her amazing beauty.

"I like bravery—and honor—even if the Magister does not!" she said, laughingly. Her almond eyes slid up and down his brawny body. "And where I like—I sometimes love," she added, her voice husky, seductive.

Chandar looked at her squarely.

"You are lovely, witch. I have seen none lovelier . . . but you cannot tempt me."

She leaned closer, the cold cups of her breast-plates just touching his bare chest.

"No . . . ?"

"No," he laughed. "If you want me, you must take Bram as well. Either that—or the arena. Take your choice."

For a long moment they looked at him: Sarkond with

puzzled, measuring eyes, Mnadis with a cool, tantalizing mockery and a certain admiration. Then—

"Take the red-beard," Sarkond said bruskly. "I have little use for him, but—give him the phial."

Mnadis moved across the cell, lifted the sleeping giant's massive head and forced the dark elixir down his throat.

"He sleeps like one dead already," she laughed.

Sarkond drew another phial from beneath his robes and gave it into Chandar's hand.

"I cast a spell on him that he should sleep, and not attempt to dissuade the Prince against us," he said.

Chandar grinned. "I begin to like you, old man! You are honest—and that is one trait I did not hope to find in a son of K'thom."

The magician made no reply. Chandar downed the fluid at a gulp, grimacing at the sour, unwholesome flavor. The Axe vanished beneath Sarkond's cloak, and, at a gesture, the cold chains snapped to again about the youth's wrists and legs.

"Farewell, for a time, Chandar of Orm!" A green glow began to envelop the sorceror and his beautiful servant. "With dawn, when the King comes to your cell, he will find you and the red-beard apparently strangled to death with your own chains. When you next see the day, it will be aboard my galley, bound for far and fabulous *Iophar!*"

Iophar! In the Land of Magic, beyond the great Wall of Ice! The land of evil spirits, whispered of by withered crones in boggle-tales to fright the young! The mysterious land from whence none had ever returned . . . Chandar struggled against the dark fog that rose to wrap about his mind. Tricked! By all the Gods—tricked!

Sarkond's stooped form dwindled into a spot of mystic green light and the sourceless illumination faded with him.

Just before Chandar sank into unconsciousness, he heard Mnadis' soft voice echo the Enchanter's words:

"Farewell, for a time, Chandar . . ."

And then sleep overtook him, and he fought no more.

3 IN QUEST OF—TERROR!

WHEN HE opened his eyes, he saw black sails bellying before a stiff morning wind, and a clear blue sky. The twin moons were pallid ghosts by day, low on the horizon.

He blinked. Was he dreaming? But no—he could hear the creak of cordage, and the shrill song of the wind in the rigging, and boom as a slackened canvas suddenly caught a full gust . . . and in his nostrils was a familiar scent . . . the stink of hot tar, the good brown smell of wood, all mixed in with the salt tang of the crisp sea air . . .

"Lad!" Bram loomed above him, dark against the bright sky. Chandar got slowly to his feet, legs bracing automatically to the expected pitch and roll of the vessel, as he clasped his friend's calloused paw . . . but the ship was riding smooth! No pitching from side to side, as she breasted the waves.

"Lad, it's like meat in an empty belly to see you again—but what scrape have you gotten us into this time?" The red-beard thumped his back heartily, but his eyes were puzzled and wary.

"I don't know, Bram," Chandar confessed. "I've saved our lives—"

"—by making a deal with the Archfiend, himself! And don't nay-say me, lad—I've seen him, the thin yellow one with a head like a skull, and green eyes burning hellfire!"

Bram cursed, wiping a hand across his mouth, tugging at his beard perplexedly. "I dozed off in the cell, and came to me senses a minute or two ago, thinking meself a passenger of the Grim Ferryman, bound across the River of Shadows! This cursed ship, lad—*it floats in the air!*"

"What? You're still drugged with the potion, Bram!" The giant took his arm and led him to the rail.

"See for yourself, lad!"

23

Chandar stared down the curving hull of smooth black wood. The ship raced above the waves, a good ten paces in mid-air, as if borne by invisible spirits. Far faster than any ship that plied Jalangir Val, t⁻ ⸱ Great Sea, it rode, while the blue waves hissed by beneath.

"Deviltry, lad, by Gondomyr's Beard! We're bound for the Isle of Witches!"

"Bound, perhaps, for something worse, Bram," Chandar said, grimly. In swift words he sketched a brief outline of his bargain with the Enchanter, and at the mention of the K'thomi's trickery and the dreaded name *Iophar,* the giant shuddered, and traced upon his hairy chest the Sign of Shesh.

"What does it all mean, lad?"

"I don't know, Bram—but I mean to find out. No sailor —corsair, merchantman, or fleet yeoman—has ever returned from the Land of Magic, and this yellow devil from the jungles thinks to sail there!"

Just then a soft voice cried from behind them:

"I see you have awakened. Now, did we keep our promise?"

Chandar spun, to see Mnadis leaning at the rail a few paces away, regarding him mockingly, a slight smile on her scarlet lips. She was breath-takingly lovely: red-gold mane blown by the wind like a rough, bright banner, and wrapped in a huge sea cloak of brown oiled leather.

He hardened himself against her beauty.

"Keep your promise? Yes—and tricked me, into the bargain."

She laughed.

"Corsair! You are surly when you arise in the morning . . ."

"Take me to your master, witch, and we'll settle this mad scheme of sailing to Iophar right now!"

She laughed, and shook her head. Tiny bells chimed as her red mane foamed over her shoulders.

"No man is my master . . . unless I give myself to him."

"Up already, eh?" The smooth voice of the wizard sounded from the aft-deck. They turned and he descended the steps slowly. "Come into the cabin, Prince of Orm.

Cleanse your wounds and break your fast. We are three hours to sea and well past the Bay of Nephelis by now."

"First we'll have a few words, sorcerer." Chandar planted his booted legs solidly and looked the yellow magician squarely in the eye.

"Words that include the name *Iophar,* I presume?" the Enchanter said, with his thin-lipped smile.

"Aye, that, and words like 'tricked' and 'trapped' and —'lied' as well!" Chandar flared.

"I have neither tricked nor trapped you, and I have not lied," the Enchanter said calmly.

"You promised to set me free and return me to the Hundred Isles—"

"Yes, I promised to do all that—if you would do me a service. And when that service has been performed, I shall indeed pay you—I shall reward you fittingly."

"What service, sorceror? To die in cursed Iophar?"

"You are no longer a child, Prince, to be frightened with whispered tales of demons and witches. Iophar is a city like any other . . . in a land ruled by magicians, that is true, but I am a magician to match their best. Have no fear."

"Don't trust him, lad. He has the tongue of a snake, that one," Bram rumbled suddenly.

"You lied when you said you would return the Axe of Orm to me," Chandar challenged, ignoring the red-beard's outburst. He jutted out his jaw, stubbornly. "I want it now."

"You shall have it in good time, Prince of Orm, I promise you that. Now go into your cabin, wash your wounds, and eat. I shall explain our quest to you when you have finished, and make plain your part in it. Now go. Girl, come with me. We have work to do."

The Enchanter turned on his heel and entered the main cabin. There was nothing else for Chandar to do, but to obey him.

It was good to wash with hot water and soothe his many stinging cuts with a cool ointment Mnadis provided. And good, too, to fill his empty middle with sharp, cold wine and bread and fruit. From a seachest he drew a brief tunic of black leather, to replace his tattered rags, and a broad leather belt studded with brass nail-heads, to clasp his waist. But weapon, there was none, and he felt uncomfortable without a blade swinging against his thigh.

The red-beard, too, relaxed somewhat with a tankard of ale in his belly. But he grimly warned Chandar: "Watch out for that wily old snake, lad. I'll step on his head for you, just give me the sign!"

"I can take care of him myself, man."

"Aye? And the red witch—can you take care of yourself with her?" the giant asked, sharply.

"I—"

"Watch yourself when that wench is about, lad! She has an eye for you—and a K'thomi wench, too, with the morals of a devil."

Chandar grinned, his blood warming. "Is that bad, Bram? Many is the time I've heard you boast over a tankard, of the golden-skinned dancers of Nomor by the Nalizar . . . and the dusky jungle girls of the Southlands. Why cavil at a girl like her?"

"Ptha!" Bram spat. "I'd sooner mate with a lizard-woman from the Black Desert. She's a witch, lad, and no doubt will soon offer you a taste of her magic."

"Oh, still your eternal growling! You're not my nursemaid now; I can handle her."

When they entered the main cabin, they saw Mnadis and Sarkond whispering together, seated at the end of a long table littered with parchment scrolls and magic implements. Chandar ran his eye around the low-ceilinged room. It was long and roomy, and at the rear wall, diamond-paned windows opened on a view of blue water and pale sky. About the curving walls were chests and low tables, whereon wood racks of glass tubes, flasks and heavy jars of colored fluids and powders were securely locked in place. A lovely armillary sphere stood at one corner of the room, its hammered copper marked with the ever-changing positions of the stars and planets, mounted on turning wheels. The room stank of sorcery.

At the long table's head, the Enchanter sat enthroned in a great carven chair of blue translucent smokestone. He sat back, abruptly ending his muted converse with Mnadis, and welcomed them with a thin-lipped smile.

Before him was a huge sheet of yellow vellum, whereon in inks of scarlet, green and black were sketched the isles and countries of the known world. A white symbol, like a stylized flame, was painted on the place where Iophar was reputed to stand.

Sarkond began the conversation with no preliminaries.

"The Axe of Orm, Prince, is more than the hereditary weapon of your House and its emblem of Kingship. None know of this but I . . . it is a talisman of magic. To speak plain truth, it is an Arch-Talisman, capable of rendering null all and any spells, cantrips, runes, enchantments or sendings whatever."

Chandar's calm face did not betray his astonishment at this amazing news, but merely nodded. The wizard smiled.

"Such information may startle you, but such is fact. And moreover, the powers locked within the very substance of the Axe cannot be loosed or directed by any, save those who bear the ancient blood of Orm within their veins. Now you see, I think, why your presence here is necessary to my plans?"

Chandar accepted a goblet of rose-crystal from Mnadis, and paused while she filled it to the brim with yellow, sparkling wine of Arviara.

"These plans of yours remain yet unexplained," he observed.

The Enchanter took a full goblet and saluted Chandar, drank, and put it down.

"Iophar is the capital of magic. Its wizards are legended to be the most powerful of all the world. The source of their power lies in something called The Flame . . . it may be an Arch-Talisman, a jewel, perhaps a ritual. I know not. But to bring my plans to fruition, I need that power."

"What plans?" Chandar repeated.

"Nothing less than to defeat the cruel imperial ambitions of that most loathsome of Kings—my enemy as he is yours," Sarkond answered smoothly. "I am a philosopher, a thinker, a man of peace. I seek only knowledge and wisdom. But Niamnon of Shiangkor threatens the peace of the world, and it is my plain duty to use what little wisdom I have learned to foil his evil schemes and free the proud cities he has enchained."

Chandar took another gulp of the cold, tingling wine. "Say on."

"Now Iophar is protected from molestation and unwanted guests by the Wall of Ice—a magically-constructed wall hundreds of leagues in length, built deep into the floor of the ocean and rising into the air thrice the height of a ship's mast. My skill cannot penetrate this enchanted barrier. Nor can I gain entry by other means. Twice in past years have I so attempted. Once by air, astride a great gryphon from the Rhazarian Mountains, tamed by my magic bridle. But mighty winds of wizardry beat my gryphon back. The second attempt was overland, from the north . . . I landed on the promontory many leagues outside the Land of Magic, and journeyed upon a magic stallion built of brass. But to the north, the Land of Magic is protected by a Wall of Fire, and my sorcerous steed could not pass. At length I took service with Niamnon of Shiangkor, for his Hall possessed a far-famed library of grimoirs and magic books, collected by his scholarly father, King Eryndax. While carrying out my pretence of loyal service, I found many occasions to seek through the tomes . . . finding at last the clue I needed. Girl, more wine for the Prince . . ."

Impatiently, Chandar waved the wine aside.

"Continue." he said.

"Very well. I learned that only an Arch-Talisman could pierce the magic Walls. Now there are but three such sigils of power in all the realms and isles of which we know. The first, called the Sword of Psamathis, is buried somewhere below that ancient city, in the crypts. But those subterranean tombs are . . . shall we say . . . terribly guarded. The second such device, a crystal of unknown powers, is lost to all knowledge . . . reputed to have vanished beneath the oceans of Polaria when that age-old and grimly legended dominion was overwhelmed and drowned by the Immortal Gods in distant ages, in punishment for some inhuman sin. The third Arch-Talisman is the Axe, and as you alone bear within your flesh the blood of Gondomyr, your life is as precious to me as to you. For that reason I rescued you from the dungeons of Shiangkor, at risk of my head. I had constructed this magic flying ship in readiness for my attempt to breach the Ice-Wall, and had

planned to seek out your corsair haven within the Hundred
Isles . . . when your untimely capture and imprisonment
made such an act unnecessary."

Chandar leaned back, a puzzled frown creasing his brow.

"Your tale intrigues me, wizard. And, may well be true.
Yet if the Axe bears any power beyond that given it to
kill, when wielded by a strong right hand, neither I nor my
House ever suspected it."

The Enchanter leaned forward intently, resting his arms
on the littered table.

"Such is, however the case. The talismanic force is
there, locked in the elements that constitute it. Were your
senses alert to magical emanations, as are mine, you would
detect the throb of its magical aura at once."

"Perhaps . . . but at any rate, I know not how to unleash this power," Chandar said, honestly.

The Enchanter shrugged. "Leave that to me. The grimoirs said the talismanic energies were sealed in the Axe by
the Kyphi Ritual, and can be directed by that rite, whose
use I know and can instruct you in. It is simpleness itself.
Would that I could use the Axe, for then I could spare you
any trace of possible danger from its unleashing. But I am
unprotected by the charm in your blood, and the back-blast
of force would rip my form to shreds."

Bram, who had been silent till now, standing behind the
Prince's chair, glowering at the faintly-smiling witch and
the old wizard, growled: "A good thing for us, K'thomi,
that you need the boy's help—or you would make fish-
meat of him in seconds. Your oily words do not slip past
me!"

The Enchanter regarded him levelly.

"Your aid, however, I have no use for, and may yet be
persuaded to dispense with, barbarian pig!"

Bram's fae flushed as scarlet as his beard.

"Barbarian pig, is it? That from a slime-bellied snake of
the jungles!"

"Calm down, man," Chandar rapped.

Bram shook off his restraining arm.

"I fear no man living, and no spirit dead! And least of
all, a walking skeleton who has as much manhood in his
dry bones as the witch, there."

Sarkond's gaunt face writhed, but he controlled himself with a visible effort. Chandar perceived, in a moment of flashing insight, that the seemingly imperturbable calm and serenity the Enchanter displayed was but a mask, hiding a seething cauldron of passions beneath its smooth exterior. He felt a momentary qualm: Sarkond's manner and soft words had half-persuaded him to believe his plausible tale! The K'thomi was a sly and subtle adversary.

The Enchanter stood. "You are ill-advised to cast your spittle at me, red bear. With a lifted hand I could blast you where you stand."

"Blast—and be damned to you! The God Who Watches Over The Sea protects his own . . . I fear no southlander magic!"

"The Lord Shesh cannot help you, should I lift my hand," said Sarkond coldly. "Prince of Orm, silence your bull-brained companion, or I shall silence him myself."

Chandar half arose—but suddenly the cabin erupted into a blaze of action. Bram turned with a roar, seizing Mnadis' slim wrist and twisting it cruelly, wringing a gasping cry from the girl. She had crept silently up behind him, as he had exchanged words with the Magister.

He crushed her slight wrist in one powerful paw, and a slim-bladed dirk fell from her fingers, ringing on the table top.

"Bowels of Drega! Knife me in the back, would you, witch?"

"My hand—!"

"Bram—stop it!" Chandar shouted.

"Ugor—"

At Sarkond's word, a door to the rear of the room crashed open, and a weird hulking form thundered into the room. The girl, Chandar and Bram froze into a strained tableau.

The thing stood eight feet high, massive of chest and trunk, with bowed waddling legs and gigantic arms as thick as Bram's hairy thigh. From a grinning, fang-edged mouth, saliva dribbled down into the thick azure fur that covered the hulking monster's entire body. Tiny red eyes flamed with murder-lust.

"Ugor—kill!"

Sarkond pointed at the gaping Bram, and the monster lunged across the cabin, rumbling with bestial fury.

"By Shesh! A blue ape of Zamanga!" Chandar gasped.

Bram roared his berserker challenge, and seized up a massive chair of heavy wood—brandishing it in one great hand, like a light wand. The blue ape crashed forward, hurling Chandar against a wall, and reached for Bram with huge clawed hands.

The chair smashed to splinters against Ugor's horned skull. For a moment the blue ape reeled, shaking his head as a thin green trickle of beast-blood seeped into his eyes.

Then he seized Bram's shoulder, his talons ripping the thick leather jerkin like thin silk—and drew the pirate within his reach. Bram swung his fist—straight to the heavy chin with a *crack!* that rocked the blue ape back on its heels, and followed with a sledge hammer punch in the creature's belly. But it was only dazed.

They grappled, roaring. Bram buried his face in the ape's chest to keep away from its fangs, and locked his arms behind the sloping shoulders. His muscles strained, fists digging into the small of the ape's back. It roared, pummeling his shoulders with might fists . . . clawing at him with razor talons that laid his leather jerkin in ribbons. Chandar's eyes glinted: Bram was trying to break the ape's back!

Then, with a bellow of rage, it broke free—hurling Bram against the table and overturning it. Mnadis shrieked.

Chandar's eye lighted on the girl's dirk. He snatched it up and sank it in the round bulge of the ape's shoulder. It went in smoothly, sliding through the thick curve of muscle. He dragged it down the arm. Blood spurted from the slash, green beast-blood that stained the thick fur and splattered on the floor.

The ape swayed, fumbled at its crippled shoulder. One arm hung motionless. Then it whirled on Chandar, ignoring Bram where he lay stunned against the over-turned table.

Chandar backed away cautiously, dirk raised to strike at the ape's throat—

4 THE RED WITCH

MNADIS TURNED to the Enchanter, who stood calmly observing as Chandar fought the blue ape. "Stop it, Magister! If he is killed, all your plans go for naught! Stop it now!"

The ape caught Chandar's hand with a huge paw, crushingly. They closed. Chandar smelled the monster's reeking breath and the hot smell of its fur against his face. He kicked the ape's bowed legs out from under it and they crashed to the floor. His head rang against an over-turned chair and the cabin swam about him, hazed in a drunken red mist—

"Ugor—back!"

The crushing weight slid off him and Chandar gasped for breath. He opened his hand and let the blade drop from nerveless fingers. His hand felt as if all the bones were crushed. The ape waddled obediently to the Enchanter.

"Perhaps you and your bullheaded companion will think twice before angering me another time," Sarkond said softly. He calmed the grunting beast, petting it and clucking to it.

Chandar staggered to his feet and looked to Bram who was coming around. The flagon of Arviaran goldwine lay on the floor still stoppered and unbroken. Chandar poured the sparkling fluid in Bram's mouth, and he spluttered, coughed, and came to, groggily.

From beneath his cloak, Sarkond drew a flat box of suave yellow cream and smeared it along the ape's slashed shoulder, muttering mystic words. The blue ape whimpered, grunted, then flexed his arm. The wound had closed and the muscle healed even as they watched. Then Sarkond glanced at the two.

"This will soothe your hurts," he said, handing the box towards Chandar.

Bram waved it away.

"None of your stinking magic," he rumbled.

"Are you all right, man?" Chandar asked.

"A few scratches, that's all. That, and a sore back where that devil-beast nearly pounded me to jelly. I'm all right."

"I regret that this unseemly incident had to occur," Sarkond said quietly. "Next time, do not vex me. Ugor is the least of my weapons."

At the sound of his name, the ape pricked his ears and snarled softly.

Sarkond led it lumbering back into its little room.

Mnadis turned swiftly to Chandar.

"Leave now," she urged. "Forget what happened. It will not occur again, if only you can keep your friend from angering him!"

Chandar nodded.

"Come on, Bram. Let's go wash those scratches."

All that day the black ship flew like some fantastic bird of wood beneath a cool blue sky. Sarkond remained locked in the main cabin, and Mnadis was nowhere to be seen. Bram drank deeply of the goldwine and then slept in his bunk, and Chandar was left to his own devices. He explored the ship from stem to stern, but found nothing of use or interest. The cabins below deck and the hold were empty, even the galley. Sarkond either conjured food and drink from thin air, or kept supplies in his main cabin. But for themselves, there were no others aboard the vessel. Then who worked the ship?

Chandar went topdecks again. It was as if invisible hands operated the black galley—sails were furled or raised, the wheel twisted, keeping her head before the wind—yet all without a visible hand at work. He shivered. Either the vessel were manned by spirits . . . or perhaps the Enchanter had invested the wood and rope and canvas with a pseudo-life and the ship operated herself. There was a thought to keep one awake nights! He grinned recklessly. Drega take the whole business.

A helpless captive on a hell-ship manned by spirits and captained by a black sorceror, bound for the edge of the world! He grinned wryly. What a saga this tale would make, for the blind harpers!

And yet . . . he expanded his lungs, drinking in the tang of salt air, the baking sun. His eyes took in the blue sparkling plain of sea, the clear sky, the soft clouds. Over his head, the canvas boomed and swelled, and swift wind sang shrilly through the spars and rigging. It was better than a dank cell beneath Shiangkor . . . and better than the reeking, blood-splattered sands of the arena. It was good to be alive, even on a devil's quest like this!

He lazed away the long afternoon, lying in the sun and letting the warmth bake through his muscles. Bram joined him on deck later, and they sat talking of old times, both deliberately ignoring the difficult situation around them. When the sky began to purple with evening and the declining sun painted the cloud-wisps with gold and scarlet, food and drink magically appeared in their cabin. There was still no sign of the old magician or the girl. They ate and the food was good—a hot, spicy stew of boiled *boupon* chunks, brown gravy and thick bread. With good sour ale to wash it down.

Still aching from his battle with the blue ape, Bram turned in. But Chandar went back on deck.

The ship ran silently now, under a dark sky where northern stars burned unwinkingly. The White Moon was aloft, but his younger brother had not yet arisen.

Chandar leaned against the rail, gazing down at the rushing water. Green phosphorescent fire swirled through the black water, and flakes of fire flashed in the blown spume.

"Dreaming, corsair?"

He raised his head. She was there, wrapped in a warm furred cloak. Her hair spread on the wind, silver bells chiming faintly, and the moonlight glistened softly along her cheek and throat.

"Perhaps. Do you not dream?"

She came to stand beside him, gazing down at the sea of dim green lambency.

"I . . . dream."

"Of what do you dream, Mnadis?"

"Sometimes I dream of my home. I was born in a little hut by the Nalizar . . . I can remember how the jungle orchids spread their perfume on such nights as this, with the great stars blazing down, and the White Moon floating, glowing like the ghost of a sun. I remember lying awake on my pallet, listening to the night-birds calling to one another in the dark . . ."

"How did you ever get into this thing, a girl like you?"

She looked at him somberly.

"How do you think, corsair? I was sold to Sarkond when I was twelve."

"Sold? To that cold devil?"

She nodded, bells chiming faintly.

"My father was poor, and hunting was bad one season. Agents came to him and offered to buy me. There were three children, and I was the loveliest. It is a common story, corsair."

"But how could you endure—"

Mnadis smiled. "The Magister has never touched me. Women do not interest him. No, he kept me for other purposes . . ."

Suddenly she turned to him.

"Listen to me, Chandar of Orm! You must not trust him. You cannot oppose him, but do not believe what he tells you. Lies come more easily to him than the truth."

"I have already discovered that for myself," Chandar said bitterly. "Is he lying about the Axe?"

"No, that is true enough. He needs you to operate the magic in the Axe, to get through the Wall of Ice, but after that . . ."

"After that, my usefulness to him has ended, is that it?"

"Yes . . ."

He reached out and took her slim shoulders in his hands.

"What does he want in Iophar?"

"I am not sure . . ."

"Not sure? Surely, you are privy to his secrets!"

She shook her head.

"Some things he keeps from me. But I know this, you must watch yourself with him. He hates you, and will not hesitate to destroy you. He is no friend of yours, regardless of what he may say."

Chandar shrugged. "I must admit he has helped me. He saved me from Niamnor, when that cursed storm threw me into the Admiral's trap, off the Bay of Nephelis. I owe him that, at least."

"You fool! Do you still think that storm was an accident?"

"What do you mean . . ."

She glared at him, passionately. "Who do you think raised that storm against yoυ, you trusting fool! Sarkond. He saw your pirate fleet in his magic glass, and raised the storm that sank and dispersed it, leaving you helpless before Kralian's squadron. Who do you think guided the Admiral to where you were? Sarkond. He is behind all your troubles."

Chandar swore.

"That yellow snake! I'll have his guts at the end of a pike for that!"

"Ah, there is nothing you can do."

"Nothing? Listen, wench. The men that died in that storm were good friends—men for whom I would have died! I'll have his heart for that, at least, before I die!"

"What can you do, corsair? He spoke truly. The ape is the least of his guardians. There are invisible spirits who serve his will—"

"When we reach the Wall of Ice—and I hold Orm's Axe in these two hands—"

"No! He will kill you!"

Chandar laughed mirthlessly. "Death and I are old comrades, we have faced each other many times—"

Suddenly, without words, she was in his arms. He smelled the spicy fragrance of her hair and her lips clung to his.

And then the ship stopped dead.

5 THE WALL OF ICE

THE SUDDEN halt hurled him against the rail, and he clung there gasping. Before the black prow a wall of glittering, glassy ice rose suddenly, taller than the tallest mast. The sails hung slack, empty of wind. Silence hung over the ship, as heavy as the fantastic wall that brooded down upon them.

Chandar raised his eyes. Above them, on the afterdeck, the gaunt form of the Enchanter stood, smiling thinly down.

Chandar stifled a curse. His blood beat thick and hot in his temples, but not from passion. He looked at the stooped K'thomi.

"Where is the Axe?"

"Here." Sarkond drew it from beneath his cloak. "Come forward, to the prow. I will show you how to use it."

Bram stumbled from the cabin, rubbing his head.

"What's happened, lad, have we rammed a sea-dragon?"

Bram took the vast glittering ice-barrier in with dazed eyes.

"Sure, and it will take more than an axe to make a passage in that!" he grumbled.

Sarkond laughed, exultantly. He seemed possessed by a sudden excitement. His eyes glared in the dim light.

"Come forward, red bear of Orm, and you shall see magic! Ah, Gods! How I have waited for this moment!"

From the prow, the Wall towered over them against the starry sky like a mighty fortress. Sarkond gave the Axe into Chandar's hands. His fingers closed over the smooth handle tightly.

"Hold it before you, thusly," Sarkond said, gesturing. "With the blade up and forward, just in front of your eyes. Ah, good—good!"

Chandar felt his spirits rise happily, with the good weight of the Axe in his hands at last. He felt more than a match for any sorceror, now.

"What next, Enchanter?" he laughed.

"Repeat the Kyphi Ritual after me," Sarkond said. And Chandar's tongue stumbled over the uncouth syllables that fell droningly from Sarkond's thin lips. The chant went on, him repeating the words as the sorceror spoke them. From the corner of his eye he could see Bram glowering, signing himself with the Sign of Shesh . . . Mnadis watching him with a fierce warning flashing in her eyes. Under the gunwales, Ugor cowered, whimpering. Chandar could see the

blue ape trembling, and wondered if the beast's senses detected some occult influence his own were blinded to—
    And then he felt it . . . a tingling life in the Axe! It
was so unexpected that he almost snatched his hands away
from the smooth handle that was suddenly warm and
quivering. The Axe shivered in his grip like a live thing
. . . and a tingling warmth went through his body. It was
like wine, singing in his blood. He felt a heady sense of
power . . . power! The Ritual was ended. Sarkond's thin
lips were silent—as if waiting for some sign. Chandar's
form seemed to expand, to tower over them. His head
swam drunkenly, then cleared. His senses sharpened—he
could see every crack and facet in the ice-wall . . . every
pore in his hands, held before his eyes. Then a swift blur-
ring of sight, and he could see through his flesh, to the
strange white bones, netted in a web of pulsing veins and
long, glossy muscles!
    "Hai! Gods!"
    He laughed, his great voice booming out like a trumpet-
call. He felt like a God standing there . . . a sense of
measureless power sang warm within him. He tasted the
wine of Omnipotence against his tongue . . . as if with
an extended hand he could form and hurl a shaft of lightning . . . as if, at a gesture, he could send tall mountains
crumbling, toppling, in a rain of boulders.
    "Lad! Be careful!" Bram shouted.
    Chandar laughed again, mockingly. How petty were
men's small fears and desires, compared to this godlike
power that roared through him now! He could feel strength,
like a seething river of force, strength building up in him.
His arm-muscles grew, swollen with power. Now a waver-
ing nimbus of pallid light grew around him—beating rays
of light illuminated the deck like a third moon. Mnadis
moaned, and shielded her eyes against the glare. Sarkond
watched through slitted eyes.
    Chandar hurled the Axe—
    It traced a flaming arc against the night, and smote the
ice cliff. The wall rang like a great gong, and the Axe
came flying back. Chandar caught it in his hand with ease.
Long black cracks spread through the ice. A tearing sound,
like great masses of crystal smashing—a grinding crunch,

as of stones being mauled and crushed. Great splinters of ice fell about them.

"Again!"

Chandar hurled the Axe a second time. Lightning sizzled about it. It hurled through the dark air like a blazing ball of magic fire—and the *Ice-Wall broke!*

With a thunderous crash, the Wall exploded. Gigantic boulders of solid ice fell away, beating the foaming sea to a churning lake of green phosphorescence. An immense tower of ice fell backward into the water, shaking the air with the impact of its collapse . . . and leaving a channel the width of the ship free of the icy barrier.

The Axe fell at Chandar's feet, smouldering. Its light faded.

Sarkond cried strange words, and the hovering ship quivered into life . . . drifting forward into the cleared channel. Walls of broken and steaming ice rose on both sides. The curved belly of the ship scraped sickeningly against jagged ice-edges.

Chandar slumped, suddenly drained of power. His senses wavered and he reeled against the rail dizzily. Numbly, he bent and picked up the Axe of Orm. It lay, a dead weight in his strengthless hand. He gasped for breath, feeling like one on the verge of fainting.

The ship slid on through the thick wall, moving effortlessly through the steaming air.

Sarkond's eyes glittered like a snake.

"You have performed your service, Prince of Orm. And now to repay you—as you deserve!"

"Wha— wha—?" Chandar gasped, struggling for strength.

From his girdle, the Enchanter plucked a weird tube of glass and metal, intricate and curious. He leveled it at Chandar's chest as the corsair watched, with dull, uncomprehending eyes—

"Snake of K'thom!"

Bram sprang! With one iron hand he seized the Enchanter's bony wrist—and with the other grasped his throat, lifting the light form over his head. Mnadis screamed!

With a coughing grunt, Ugor hurled upon him, bearing the red beard to the deck. They tumbled, struggling. Sarkond was hurled to the deck with a thin cry. And slowly raised himself, eyes blazing with mad fires.

Bram kicked the blue ape in the belly with one booted foot. The ape rolled away, snarling and Bram grabbed up a heavy belaying pin.

Sarkond limped across the deck to pick up the glass-and-metal implement, that lay where it had fallen in a pool of moonlight. Reflections from the moving wall of ice cast flickering small lights over the scene. Chandar still clung to the rail, fighting for consciousness, watching the battle with dazed eyes.

The Enchanter lifted the glass rod and pointed it at Bram's back. He spoke a whispered word . . . and a ball of soft violet fire formed in the haft of the tube and floated down its length . . . drifting out across the deck . . . struck and clung to Bram's broad back. The giant stiffened as if a bolt of electric force had gone through him. His mouth fell open, though he made no sound . . .

Chandar fought for strength. Dizzily, he raised the Axe, summoning his strength.

The ball of purple light entered Bram's body, soaking in like a drop of water on a sponge. The giant stood, paralyzed. And Sarkond laughed again, a thin cutting edge of mirth.

Ugor roared—and charged the helpless, frozen giant.

Chandar moved—and the Axe of Orm entered the ape's brow, splitting his snarling face in half. The Axe sank to the jaws. The ape tottered, his head a sudden rush of green blood, and fell to the deck like a fallen log, rolling into the gunwales.

Sarkond screamed!

He seemed to go mad with rage. He struck out, slapping the corsair across the face. Weakened still, Chandar fell flat and lay, unable to rise. Sarkond towered over him, eyes flaming.

"For that, dog of Orm, you shall die—slowly!" he hissed, his pointed tongue flickering snakelike between grinning lips. He drew another implement from his girdle, a chain of tiny links. Pressing a sigil against the chain he watched as it glowed with sudden red fire.

"Magister—*no!*"

"Silence, wench! He has served his purpose—and slew. Ugor! It is time we cleansed our ship of this scum of foulness."

The glowing chain snapped and slithered in his hands, alive with energy. Chandar watched it, dully. The Enchanter held it over his bare, heaving chest.

"When it touches your flesh, it will cling and burn like red-hot metal, crawling over you like a snake of fire! Know then, the strength of Sarkond, you cur of Orm!"

Then Mnadis was upon him, spitting and clawing like a jungle *thanth*. She clawed at his eyes, dragging him over backward. The slithering chain fell to the wooden deck, charring the planks. Sarkond cursed, and slapped her off.

"You too, girl? Then I have a special death for you, as well!"

Chandar struggled to rise to his feet, but his last dregs of strength had been drained by his effort to hurl the Axe at the Zamangan ape. He was completely helpless.

Sarkond cuffed the witch away, and snatched up with bare hands the wriggling, smoking chain of red-hot metal. He seemed immune to the effects of his own sorcery, for he showed no pain as the blazing, smoking chain curled and writhed around his bare wrist. He strode over towards Chandar, his face working with rage, a livid, deathly-pale mask of hatred.

At that moment the Wall of Ice closed.

Ponderous jaws of ice closed upon the ship, cracking it from end to end like a nutshell, with a dreadful crunch. Masts snapped off—wood crunched and splintered. Unable to move a muscle, Chandar fell into the icy shock of death-cold black water. He sank like a stone. Cold water filled his mouth, crushing his lungs. The chill shock brought a rush of sudden strength back into his limbs . . . choking for breath, he struck out with arms and legs, wildly.

He was strangling for want of air . . . blackness closed about him. Blind and deaf, his lungs screaming for air, he kicked madly against the cold water, as at an enemy.

This his head broke water. He sucked air into his lungs, and tossed the wet hair out of his eyes. Treading water, he looked around him. The churning phosphorescence of the water cast a dim green blur of light upon a nightmare scene.

The Wall had closed again, crumpling the ship like a piece of parchment crushed in a closed fist. A shattered tangle of broken boards and spars projected from the Wall, and a tangle of splintered wreckage hung down into the water, which was a swirling mass of wood and ripped sail-cloth. As he watched, the ice closed a little more, and the main mast snapped off short. It crashed into the sea of icy water, sending flying showers of fire-flakes and hurling bits of broken wood into the air. The ice ground together with a dull grating sound.

Chandar could feel the icy chill of the water sink numbingly into his bones. The strength was leaving him again. He swallowed black water, choked, and flailed, beating the foam. A spar floated near, and clinging to it he saw the form of Mnadis, her body glistening with phosphorescence. She did not see him—her fascinated gaze was fixed on something far above—he tried to call her, but his voice was a rasping croak and he swallowed more water. His senses began to blur. He saw Bram's body, hung crazily over a jutting angle of the ice.

Then a weird, metallic cry came from the star crowded sky. He looked up, and saw the thing that Mnadis stared at—

A dragon, winged and clawed, a scarlet snaky body floating on the wind, like the emblem of the flags of Shiangkor!

It hovered above them with beating wings, and there, mounted upon its back was a girl . . . a girl . . . her pearly body shrouded in clinging veils of soft white lace . . . with flying hair like soft yellow gold and huge blue eyes that stared down at him . . .

He was dead, and she was a War-Maid come to bear him off to the Hall of Heroes . . . he was dreaming, and she was only a vision of his weary mind . . . now the dragon, at her ringing word, sank towards him with beating vans, fanning flakes of fire from the foaming waves.

Then consciousness left him completely, and he sank into the cold water again.

6 CAPTIVES—IN THE LAND OF MAGIC

CHANDAR WAS dead. Utter darkness surrounded him like black smoke and he floated in space, unmoving, unthinking. Then—a call, faint, pure, singing—and he felt himself begin to rise. The mists faded from black to purple about him as he drifted up . . . and up. He did not want to rise. He wanted to remain in the bosom of blackness, sleeping without dreams . . . but the faint, clear call came again. Now the swirling mists flushed with red . . . lacy coils of utter scarlet foamed and broke about his floating form. And as he rose, the whirling mists yellowed towards gold, paled into cream, and cleared into soft, fleecy white. The call was very near now, beating upon him like some strange bird-song . . . it was very sweet and cool. The mists about him were now a thin vapor of pure, soft white light . . .

He opened his eyes, and looked at her.

She was so lovely that it went through him like a pain. Her face was a calm oval, with dreaming lips of pale coral, warm and soft and . . . child-like. Her incredible eyes were the sweet blue of corn-flowers, shadowy under thick lashes. All about her fell tides and cataracts of golden hair, hiding her slim shoulders and veiling her breast. Child-like, too, was her soft voice as she sang, her white hands striking faint strains of delicate music from a small lute of gold, which she held on her lap. Her hands played upon it, caressingly. Looking without conscious thought, he saw that her white wrists were slender as bird's throats.

"That is a lovely song," he said.

She smiled, and her face flushed delicately.

"You are awake! Oh, I am glad. You slept so very long . . ."

He looked around him. He was lying in a bed soft as any cloud. A delicious warmth and lassitude possessed him.

43

Gone was the biting cold of black water, the weakness of drained limbs. He felt at ease, at peace. The room in which he lay was filled with dim soft light. The walls were pearly, nacreous, curved. The ceiling was a smooth hollow, and there were no windows. It was like being in the heart of a pearl, he thought sleepily.

"Am I dead?" he asked, without really caring.

She laughed, a ringing peal like little bells.

"Do you feel—hear—see?" she asked.

"I see you," he said. "And you are like a maid of Paradise."

Her beautiful eyes flashed with mischief.

"You are not dead, nor in Paradise. You have slept—slept a long while—so that your hurts might heal and your body rest."

"Is this—Iophar?"

"Yes, it is the City of the Flame," she said. She rose, a lithe movement, and shook her golden tides of hair back over smooth shoulders. She was gowned in pure white lace, fragile as a wisp of vapor, beautiful as a dream. Sweet virginal breasts lifted the fabric tightly, and it molded to long thighs and legs when she moved.

"Don't go," he said.

"I must bring you something to eat," she said. A portion of the curved, glistening wall melted and re-formed behind her.

Iophar . . .

Experimentally, he tested his limbs. Everything seemed sound. He sat up, expecting his head to reel dizzily, but he felt superb, fit, glowing with health. Well, if this was the city of demons, he would not be satisfied with Paradise! He smiled at the thought.

When she entered the chamber again, he was standing beside the bed and she hurriedly set a small tray down on a little, low table.

"Oh, you must lie down! You are not strong enough."

"I feel fine—" he said, and even as the words were spoken, his knees buckled beneath him and he sat down suddenly on the edge of the bed. She helped him back between the sheets, and plumped soft pillows behind his back.

"You must still rest awhile," she chided. "And drink this, it will give you strength." She lifted a fragile goblet of rose-tinted eggshell-thin crystal to his lips. He drank a warm, spicy fluid that tasted good going down, and that spread into a sphere of warmth in his middle.

"You are a wonderful nurse," he said sleepily.

"Shush. You must sleep again."

"You are . . . beautiful, so beautiful," he said.

She flushed a warm coral, and veiled her eyes behind thick lashes. But he saw that her pure lips curved in a soft smile. And then he was asleep.

When he woke again hours, or days, later, she was not there. He felt perfect. Energy tingled through every limb and muscle. He got out of bed, and noticed with surprise that he was nude. Had he been so . . . when he'd gotten up before? When *she* was there? He flushed at the thought.

Beside the bed, on the low table where she had put down her tray, he saw his tunic and belt of black leather, and hurriedly slipped into them. And beside the bed, leaning against it was—

The Axe!

He grunted with surprise, and picked it up, hefting its weight. How came it here? It should have sunk with the ship . . . and how, now that he thought of it, came he here? He should have been drowned . . .

Or was the scarlet dragon not a dream? He grunted, suddenly remembering the girl with golden hair floating upon the icy wind, that he had glimpsed seated between the dragon's beating wings—she was the same girl who had nursed him, the girl with cornflower-blue eyes . . .

Chandar shrugged. Dream or reality, it mattered not. He was alive. He was here, here in—Iophar. And were the others alive as well—Sarkond and Mnadis?"

He went to the wall and, tucking the Axe into his girdle, he felt along it. He could not see the door she had opened, but it must be there . . .

"So you are strong enough to stand?"

The deep voice which sounded behind him caused him to spin about, landing on the balls of his feet in an instinctive fighting crouch, and the Axe leaped into his hand, ready for action. Then he relaxed, for standing beside the bed was a tall, grey-bearded old man, smiling warmly at him. Erect, vigorous although clearly of advanced years, and—unarmed.

The elder chuckled.

"Did I startle you? Forgive me. But I am happy to see that you have recovered your strength."

"How did you—"

The elder raised one lean hand, displaying a curiously massive ring of dark red stone.

"The doors of Iophar open to the bearers of such rings as this," he said camly. "But let me introduce myself . . . I am Meliander, Elder of the Council and Chamberlain to the Lady Llys, our Queen."

Chandar introduced himself, and then his brow puckered. *Meliander* . . . the name had an echo of familiarity to it. But he could not quite recall . . . yes!

"There was a certain Prince Meliander, elder brother to the King of Shiangkor," Chandar ventured. The Elder smiled.

"I am that man. Once, many years ago, I was Meliander, King of Shiangkor, until Niamnon my younger brother deposed me, seized my throne and sent me forth into exile."

Chandar's lips twisted in a thin, bitter smile.

"We are brothers in misfortune, then, Lord. For I too . . ."

Meliander nodded, gravely. "I know your story, Prince Chandar. Niamnon is . . . well, let us only say, my brother is ambitious and . . . without scruple. But—misfortune! I cannot quite agree. When I fled before the assassins of the new King of Shiangkor, I came here into the north and found haven in Iophar. Here I have found a new life, among a friendly people. The Iophari are not such ogres as our legends paint them . . . their remoteness and the Wall of Ice that protects the Land of Magic lends to their name a certain air of unfriendliness, which is not borne out in their actions."

"I have already found that to be true," Chandar grinned. "I awoke to find myself tended by the loveliest nurse that ever brought succor to an ill man."

"Nurse?" Meliander looked puzzled.

"A young girl with long golden hair, bright as the sunlight. And eyes, enormous eyes of purest blue . . ."

"Ah, yes, I know your nurse." Meliander smiled covertly. "But come, we are expected. Our Queen and the Council expect you and your three companions—"

"Three? But Bram is—"

"No, he is not dead. Not—now."

Chandar felt a chill wind of uneasiness brush his flesh. "Not now?"

Meliander took his arm.

"Come, the Queen is waiting. Your friend has been revived by means of the Flame. All will be explained in due time."

Chandar shook his head. Mysteries beclouded his mind, but for the moment he must shrug them off. He little knew what to expect from these Iophari . . . but he would soon know!

The grey-robed Elder led him over to the wall and raised his right hand as the golden-haired girl had done, resting it palm down against the smooth, nacerous substance that did not seem to be wood, stone, metal or even glass. The strange curved wall *melted* before his eyes— faded into pearly vapor and simply ceased to exist. He blinked—rubbed his eyes—and blinked again. Where a square, door-shaped portion of the solid wall had been was now—nothing.

"A bit of the fabled magic of Iophar?" he asked.

Meliander nodded. "You will see many strange things here. But nothing to fear. Yes, this is truly the Land of Magic!"

They went through the portal and out into a curving hall of softly glowing blue and rose stone in alternate huge slabs. When Meliander was a certain distance from the wall, it reformed behind them, smooth and unbroken.

Chandar ran his hand over it, and laughed.

"No wonder I could not find a crack! And I remember now, that when my nurse left me to fetch some wine the 'door' seemed to melt before her, and then reform . . . I did not think much about it, still being fogged with sleep."

"Come, follow me. Your comrades await you in the Hall of Kings."

They went down the blue and rose corridor, and thence down a vast staircase whose steps were broad enough to hold a score of men marching abreast, and into a vast hall with high arched ceiling like a cathedral. The walls were dimly golden and made of some glassy substance that bore, like phantom witch-lights within their very fabric, glittering mists of tiny points of light. A crowd of curiously gowned men and women awaited them, the men in long formal robes and the women garbed in costumes of lace or foamy gauze, with puffed and tagged sleeves to their slim wrists and tiny graceful spire crowns of a dull white metal. These were perhaps the peers and nobles of Iophar. Chandar could see no weapons . . . nor did any guards stand within the hall. The floor was tiled in octagonal plates of jewel colors, and here and there along the walls, arched doorways hung with glittering fabrics opened into antechambers.

At the end of the Hall of Kings an eight-stepped dais of black marble rose beneath a tall canopy of silvercloth, bearing an empty throne of transparent crystal. Robed elders stood conferring in muted whispers upon the steps of the dais. And before the throne, waiting, stood Sarkond, Mnadis and—Bram!"

The red-beard broke into huge grins, and pummeled Chandar's shoulder, crushing his hand in a mighty grip.

"Lad—lad! They told me you were well and hardy, but I would not believe it till I saw you with these two eyes! Ah, it warms my blood to see you!"

"And they told me you were—dead," Chandar said, slapping the red-beard's burly shoulder. Bram sobered.

"Aye, we are truly in the Land of Magic, lad! Old grey-hair over there, the chief Elder, was beside my bed when I awoke. That filthy scum of K'thom had killed me, sure enough, with his cursed magic—but the Iophari brought me back from the Hall of Heroes! I tried to pry more out of him, but he's devilishly close-mouthed, that one. All he would say was—'the Flame'. But here I stand, and there stands our K'thomi friend as cool as you please. And your red-haired witch!"

Sarkond stood tall and aloof, hands folded beneath his cloak. He did not deign to give them a glance. His eyes were upon the empty throne above them.

Mnadis shot an eager, laughing glance. She would have run to him, perhaps, but the K'thomi seized her wrist and hissed sharp words into her ear, at which she dropped her head and did not meet his eyes again.

At that moment a silvery blast sounded from invisible trumpets, and the drapes at the back of the canopy parted to reveal a tall, slim figure gowned in soft white robes.

"The Lady Llys, Queen of Iophar in the Land of Magic, Priestess of the Flame!" the massed elders chanted in solemn chorus.

They bowed low in silence.

"Please rise," a soft voice said from above.

When Chandar raised his eyes to the no-longer-empty throne of crystal, he met demurely smiling eyes the color of cornflowers, in a soft oval face of delicate white, framed in long hair of sunshine-gold. He felt a shock rip through him, and his mouth fell open.

His nurse—the girl whose beauty he had so familiarly remarked upon—was Queen of Iophar!

7 LLYS

SHE GAVE a tinkling laugh, and Chandar, feeling very stupid, closed his mouth. For a moment her eyes laughed into his, then dropped as she restrained her little smile.

Bram cleared his throat, giving Chandar a sidewise quizzical glance. And Mnadis' glance was anything but quizzical—it blazed. Chandar felt distinctly uncomfortable.

Llys began without preamble:

"Strangers are not welcome within these borders, unless invited, or unless their reasons be sound. We are interested in learning what your reasons were. Who is chief among you?"

Her eyes rested on Chandar, but Sarkond spoke smoothly in the interval, giving another low bow.

"Lady Queen, I am chief here. It was my ship that your Wall of Ice destroyed."

Her eyes touched him curiously. "You are of K'thomi blood. What does K'thom desire of Iophar?"

Sarkond smiled blandly.

"Wisdom, Lady! We of K'thom are philosophers, sages —students, if you will, of the arcane sciences. The love of learning called me to your lovely land. For all my days I have heard of your mighty city, and of the deep wisdom in the arts of magic that your people possess. I come as a humble student, asking only to sit at the feet of your wise sages."

An appreciative murmur ran about the room, and Chandar saw smiles here and there among the crowd. *The sly devil's putting it over again!* Chandar thought.

Bram was of the same feeling. From the corner of his mouth he muttered to Chandar: "That yellow snake could charm the coins out of a tightfist's purse, with words alone! But he'll sing a different chant, when we speak up and tell him what we know, eh lad!"

"And these others?" Lly's eye rested on Mnadis, Bram and Chandar. The Enchanter shrugged.

"The girl is my slave. She assists me in my researches. As for the others . . . they are scum, hired mercenaries. I saved them from prison where they had been condemned to the arena for their crimes, as I needed strong backs to assist my journey."

Bram exploded.

"You lying dog! Mercenaries, are we? Criminals?"

Sarkond cut in: "You deny you were condemned for piracy, by the King of Shiangkor? Surely you will not attempt to claim you were not members—aye, and ringleaders too—of the corsair fleet of the Hundred Isles?"

Bram spluttered: "Well—we—"

"And that you were taken by the Admiral of Shiangkor, and sentenced to the arena for your sins?"

"I—well, that's true, but—"

"Be quiet, Bram." Chandar laid a restraining hand on Bram's brawny arm. The red-beard subsided, rumbling

and muttering curses. Sarkond turned a contemptuous back
upon them and faced the Queen with a thin-lipped smile.

"Common criminals, condemned pirates," he shrugged.
"I rescued them partly because I felt sorry for them—
death in the arena is a cruel door to take to the Land of
Shadows. And because I had need of their knowledge of
seamanship."

Llys gazed at Chandar with a trace of disappointment
and—was it sadness—in her gaze.

Meliander spoke up, during the Queen's silence.

"How did you enter the Wall of Ice?"

A thin smile flickered across Sarkond's lips.

"I am not, my Lord, unlearned in magic! We of K'thom
have our arts, too, inferior as they may be to yours. When
your ice-wall closed upon my magic flying galley, I had
nearly penetrated—" He broke off, as a swift murmur of
surprise ran through the elders and Sarkond smiled again.
"Yes! I have devised a vessel that flies above the water,
rather than cutting through it. It is far more rapid than
any ship that plies the seas of Iridar. Perhaps we can exchange magical knowledge . . ."

Meliander stroked his grey beard.

"A ship that flies is great magic, indeed."

Sarkond purred: "It is nothing, elementary. Far in the
south grows a type of *seraeli*-wood which when ensorceled
by certain cants and placed under the influence of certain
sigils which align the nature of the wood to astrologic
forces—repels water, rather as one pole of the lodestone
repels another."

"Interesting, indeed. Perhaps we would find it fruitful
to exchange knowledge for knowledge. But, since your
ship does not sail the seas but, instead, the skies, what
need had you for the lore of common . . . and criminal
. . . mariners?"

Llys raised her eyes and listened closely.

The wily Enchanter shrugged again, glancing at Chandar
and Bram disdainfully.

"Even though it does not touch the waves as other ships
do, my flying galley still employs the same motive force:
the winds of heaven. I needed their sea lore to pilot me.
Now that I am here, however, they may as well be de-

livered over to your justice, my Lord—and my Lady Queen. For criminals they are, and murderers as well. If left free to their own devices in your mighty city, I have no doubt they will turn to thievery—if not worse."

Mnadis turned furiously upon him.

"No! He is mine, the black-haired Ormling!"

Llys rose, imperially.

"This audience is—ended."

And she was gone.

"I don't know what ails you, lad!"

They were at dinner. The evening stars burned clear and cold through the transparent ceiling of Meliander's chambers, where the Elder was host to Bram and Chandar.

Chandar picked moodily at his food. Bram gulped down a slim goblet of strange green wine, and waved a fat leg of roasted *tengri* at the Prince.

"First it's the red wench—and now I don't know what! Sure we're in trouble—in trouble up to our necks, unless this good Lord believed our story. But I've never seen you like this, pale as a green boy. Arrgh! I wish we'd never seen that yellow snake-face! Would to Shesh we were back in Corsair's Haven, with all the lads again!"

Meliander fixed grave eyes on Bram. A strange liking had sprung up between them, dissimilar though they were on many points.

"Have no fears of that, friend Bram! Not only do I believe your tale, but I know it to be true."

Bram stared at him, then burst out in a huge smile.

"Well, that's the first good news I've heard in ages! My Lord, you make new men of us—eh lad? But—how do you know? I mean, our words are true, but—?"

Meliander rose and strode over to the wall, where long drapes of deep purple hung from crystal ceiling to floor.

"I, who was once King of Shiangkor, am now the greatest Mage of Iophar . . . although there is one greater even than I, the Priestess of the Flame, herself. Here is how I know the truth of your tale!"

At his gesture, the curtains drew aside, revealing a circular mirror of clouded grey glass, set flush into the smooth stone wall. Within its mystic depths, tiny veils of faintly glowing mist fell endlessly.

"This is my greatest accomplishment—The All-Seeing Eye. A magic mirror which, at command, yields the simulacrum of any event taking place upon all the surface of Iridar! By its aid I have kept close watch on Shiangkor and her greedy King, my younger brother. I watched while Niamnon's fleet crept into the fjords below Ormsgard . . . when you bore off the youth, Chandar, into exile in the Hundred Isles, my eyes were upon you . . . and I observed how you two welded the corsairs into a disciplined navy of pirates, and harried the coasts of Shiangkor's growing little empire. It was sufficient to me to watch . . . I had no intent to intervene. For I have surrendered my kingly ambitions, and now in my last years, I am content to seek out and master one by one the many mysteries of Nature. I know you are not criminals in anything but the letter of the law."

Chandar spoke, the first time in an hour.

"Does . . . the Queen know?"

"No. I, only, possess the secret of the All-Seeing Eye. It is here for her to use if she wills, but my Lady has never been interested in the outside world. She is only interested in . . . the Flame."

"You will—tell her, I trust?"

"Trust me, Prince. But . . ." the old man broke off, eyes brooding.

"Yes?" Chandar prodded.

"My Lady is moody, a woman of caprice. Girl, rather, for her years are no more than yours, my Prince. Like all young women, she is given to whim—to a momentary urge. I fear that the sly words of that child of K'thom have turned her against you . . . and I had hoped . . ."

Chandar felt a flush rise in his cheeks.

"Yes? Hoped . . . ?"

Meliander met his questioning gaze squarely.

"I shall not say just what I had hoped, when I saw her look at you . . . for now in your eyes I read something of the same hope." He chuckled. "But fear not, my Prince! I shall not let that sly manipulator of words persuade her to destroy you. Trust me, and let Time work his grey, slow magic."

Chandar looked puzzled.

"I'm not sure I understand your words, but . . . I thank you."

Meliander raised a protesting hand.

"You thank me for nothing, boy! To earn your thanks I should offer you something more useful . . . for example, I could mention that my garden, just below, is very beautiful by the light of the two moons . . . and that my fire-lilies are very beautiful and fragrant on nights like these . . . so much so, that my Lady, the Queen, often visits my gardens on such nights, to taste the perfume of my fire-lilies—*wait!* My Prince! Take this ring—you cannot get through the portals without it!"

Night stretched a darkly purple wing over Meliander's garden, and stars glittered like jewels of hoar frost where they were thickly sprinkled, as from the prodigal hand of Caliara, the Lady of Stars. The Yellow Moon was high in the west and the White Moon hovered between the soaring spires of Iophar, as if impaled upon their peaks. The gold and silver moonlight cast the garden into a mystic confusion of double shadows and deep wells of blackness. Flower scent drifted on the cool night air, and caged nightingales sang throbbing music.

Chandar wandered through the garden, until he came upon a slim white figure standing by the curved alabaster brink of a pool. Phosphorescent fish swam through dark green water, with feathery trails of faint green fire behind them.

"My Lady?"

She turned suddenly, her golden hair catching fiery glints of moon, a slim white hand at her throat.

"I did not mean to startle you . . ."

"Does the Lord Meliander allow known criminals to wander loose in his gardens? When you were admitted into his custody, it was to keep you from the presence of the two K'thomi against whom you hold a grudge and might attempt to murder. I did not make him your warden so that you might wander loose!"

Her voice was clear and cool, aloof, almost cold.

"I am no criminal, Queen," Chandar said bluntly. "I am the rightful King of Orm—"

"I know, I know." She lifted a hand wearily. "The K'thom warned me you might use those lies. He told me of your pretences to the throne of Orm . . . wherever Orm might be!"

Chandar stepped nearer, his tall form dark in the light of the two moons.

"Trust him not, Lady. He is a creature of lies and deceits, a master of treachery and deception."

She turned from him, where fire-lilies burned warm crimson and hot flame-yellow on the darkness of a long-leaved bush. Plucking one, she held it against her cheek, the soft light warm against her flesh as fire-glow.

"He deceived his master, Shiangkor's King, to set me loose. He deceived me, saying he wished to oppose the King's mad schemes of world-conquest, when all he wanted was the Axe of Orm. And he will attempt to deceive you. He is here to learn the secret of this thing called the Flame."

"The Axe of Orm?" she inquired coolly. "What is that?"

"It is an Arch-Talisman, of the only three left on all this planet. It is the hereditary weapon of the House of Orm, whose heir and rightful King I am." He smiled bitterly. "Or has he already so poisoned you with his sly words, that any word I speak you do not believe?"

"How can I believe? How do I know what is truth, amid all these lies and counter-lies?"

"Did you believe me, that time in the room of pearl when I awoke from my sleep, when I said you were lovely?"

Her voice was the faintest whisper.

"Am I lovely?"

"You are very lovely, Lady of Iophar . . ."

The moonlight glittered upon the water as she drew the blazing flower across its surface, rippling the dark waters and leaving flakes of fire.

"Am I as lovely as the K'thomi girl with her golden skin?" she asked suddenly.

Chandar floundered.

"Why . . . of course . . . far lovelier!"

She turned to face him squarely, her blue eyes enormous in the pallor of her face.

"Who is she? What is she to you?"

"Why, a . . . a friend, just a friend . . ."

"A—friend."

"We are almost strangers . . . I hardly . . ."

"Then why did she say you were hers? *Are* you hers?"

"She . . . she desires me. We are not . . . lovers." Chandar blundered, stumbling over his tongue. He was glad it was dark, so she could not see the hot flush mantling his cheeks.

Llys drew away, turning her slim and regal back to him.

"Do all women desire you, pirate?" she asked, coolly. "Do you perhaps fancy that I am one of them? Is that why you seek me out in the romantic darkness of a moonlit garden?"

Chandar remained silent.

She threw away the fire-lily. It traced a long scarlet curve against the night, dripping fire.

"If you do not remain within your quarters, I will have you and your companion imprisoned. Tomorrow at the ninth hour you and your companions will meet before the Council."

Words lay thick upon Chandar's tongue, but before he could utter them he was alone in Meliander's garden.

8 THE COUNCIL OF WIZARDS

IT WAS a night of many dreams. A restless night, in which two faces rose from the shadows . . . Mnadis, with her lithe body panther-golden, and mocking eyes beneath the brazen tides of scarlet hair . . . and the calm face of Llys, enormous azure eyes, demure lips, slim white limbs veiled in a froth of lace . . . and sometimes between the two faces, Chandar in his troubled dreams saw the sallow skull-head of Sarkond the Enchanter, whose imperturbable mask hid an unknown purpose . . . called *The Flame*.

What was this thing called the Flame? Talisman—book
—ritual? A weapon, or a treasure? Why was Llys called
"Priestess of the Flame"?

He tossed and turned all night, disturbed by enigmatic
and conflicting thoughts. When morning rose, and he and
Bram broke their fast at Meliander's table with bread and
fruit and warm spiced wine, he put it to the Elder.

Meliander absently traced a pattern on the table's top
with a wine-wet finger.

"That question, my Prince, is the Queen's to answer
—if she will. I can say nothing, except that the Flame is
the fountainhead of all the power and impregnability of
Iophar . . . and the source of her Mage's wisdom. Ask
me no more, for I am sworn on this."

They were no sooner finished with the meal than a young
page came to summon the three to council. They left the
Palace and rode across the city, accompanied by an escort-
of-honor.

In the open air, Chandar's troubled spirits lifted and
lightened. It was a lovely morning, clear and bright. The
air was fresh and warm, with a hint of the salty tang of
the open sea. It was the first look he had been able to take
of Iophar, for he had been brought into the city unconscious, and by night. He had in his time seen white Delphontis amid her olive groves, and proud Shiangkor with
her copper roofs and yellow towers clinging to steep cliffs
. . . but Iophar was something different.

Incredibly tall and slender spires broke from clusters of
bubble-round domes, winging above them like slim spears.
Broad streets lined with ancient trees . . . forums and
marketplaces, at whose center groups of statuary, or great
fountains, stood. Palaces and mansions, whose chaste lines
and bare simplicity conveyed a feeling of dignity in strong
contrast to the ornate stone fantasies he had seen before.

And the wizards of Iophar had conjured forth alien
substances to work their architectural dreams into reality.
Strange glassy stuffs, smooth and cool as marble—yet often
translucent, or clear as crystal. Chandar saw no stone-
work he recognized, but the city blazed with substances
of strange color . . . arches of silver-blue that glittered
like some unrusting metal . . . domes huge beyond be-

lief, yet glass-clear . . . tessellated pavements of jewel bright yellows, greens and purples.

He shook his head in wonder. The City Beyond the Sky, where dwelt the Gods of his pantheon in their supernal splendor, could be no more beautiful than this glittering capital of the Land of Magic!

The Hall of Mages was a long colonnaded building, the faint, elusive pink of sunset clouds, set in green gardens adjacent to the College of Scribes, where, Meliander informed them, the great Library of Parelon was kept.

They dismounted, left their steeds in the care of liveried grooms, and mounted a curving stair of mistgrey stone. Great columns framed a door of silvered bronze, and within they found a great stone table in the shape of a triangle. Three sides of the table were set with thrones whereon the sages and elders of the Kingdom sat in state . . . and at the far peak of the three-sided table, a crystal chair stood empty, waiting for the Queen.

Meliander led them within the hollow triangle, where Sarkond and Mnadis stood waiting.

Llys entered by a far door.

Today she wore close-fitting silks, white and shimmering. Crowning her masses of golden hair, a delicately wrought coronet rested, all loops and whorls of silvery wire. She evaded Chandar's gaze and sat quietly.

"Sarkond of K'thom, step forward."

The Enchanter approached the table.

"When your ship was detected by Lord Meliander's magic glass, and was observed to have penetrated the Wall of Ice, we rescued your party from the sea and brought you and your people to our city by means of our tame dragon-steeds . . ."

As Llys proceeded to interrogate the Enchanter, Mnadis edged close to Chandar, so near that one rounded shoulder touched his arm. He looked sideways into her hot green eyes, an uncomfortable warmth rising in his blood.

It was the first time in . . . it seemed like ages . . . that he had been close to her. The impudent witchery of her beauty stirred him even against his will.

"Corsair! Leave off staring at that milky wench and listen. Sarkond intends to befool these bearded idiots into giving him the secret of the Flame. He can be persuasive when he wishes, as you have discovered before this."

"Why does he want it?"

Her whisper was touched with mockery.

"Power. What did you think? Surely you did not swallow his pretty fables of using the Flame against the imperial ambitions of Shiangkor! Whatever the Flame is, it gives its possessor the greatest magical power in the world . . . by its means, the Magister plans to overthrow Shiangkor and seize the throne himself. Then, kingdom by kingdom, all Iridar will fall into his hands."

Chandar mused. This was just about what he had himself believed.

"Why tell me this—tell the Queen."

Her eyes clouded.

"I cannot. I am bound to him by . . . my tongue is bound to silence. And she would not believe me."

"What can I do?" Chandar's lips twisted bitterly in a little self-mocking smile. "She would not believe me, either!"

Mnadis' grin was impudent.

"In truth? Drega! It does not look that way to me. Ever since we began whispering, the wench has been glaring at us, with glances like arrows. But listen! I have a means to leave this place, and I can take you with me—"

His glance was quizzical.

"How can we leave? Steal one of the Queen's scarlet dragons?"

"I have a certain magic . . . Sarkond knows not of . . . but you must decide *now*. Come with me, or—"

"Chandar of Orm!"

The Queen's voice was cool and sharp. He hastily looked up.

"My Lady Queen?"

"Please step forward."

He left Mnadis and came forward to stand beside Sarkond. The Enchanter did not look at him, but stood aloofly, hands tucked under his cloak.

"You are the pirate who navigated the K'thomi ship into these waters? Or was it your red-bearded companion?"

Before Chandar could speak, Sarkond smoothly interrupted.

"As I have warned you, my Lady Queen, the man is a rebel, a convicted criminal, and a liar. Is it really necessary to have such scum present during a council of such import as this?"

"My lord of K'thom! You have explained that your intentions in visiting our realm are peaceful ones—that you seek only wisdom into the laws of magic. However, we of Iophar are not unsuspicious of those who enter the Land of Magic by force, craft or stealth. Certain outsiders, such as the Lord Meliander here, on my right, entered by permission. But we must discern your motives."

Sarkond shrugged. "I am considered a master of magic in what you refer to as 'the outside world.' You of Iophar are reputed of superior knowledge in the art. What could be more natural than that I should seek to perfect myself here? Surely my invention of the flying galley proves my sorcerous powers."

Meliander raised an eyebrow.

"We have only your word that you are a Mage: your ship was unfortunately destroyed, when the Ice-Wall reformed."

Chandar broke in: "My Lady, and my Lords, I can tell you of this man's motives—"

Sarkond laughed, coldly.

"If proof of my Magisterhood is required—*behold!*"

One yellow hand snaked from behind the dull green robe and struck Chandar lightly upon the throat. Words died in his mouth. He struggled to speak, but by some spell or sigil, the power of speech had been taken from him.

Bram roared, and lunged forward.

"—And behold again!" Sarkond touched a device suspended from his girdle, and the hurtling figure of the redbeard stopped short, frozen in mid-air, motionless as a statue.

The Enchanter turned a suave gaze upon the Council . . . but whatever reaction he had desired to wring—awe, admiration or surprise—came not. They smiled faintly, and the Queen's laughter tinkled through the great Hall.

"How impressive! And now watch . . . you enchanted

the corsair with a single touch . . . I shall disenchant him without even speaking a word." She fixed the pellucid gaze of her huge eyes on the speechless Ormsling, and the spell vanished.

Chandar laughed, plucking the Axe of Orm from his belt.

"It seems that for once you have found a corner of the world in which you are no Magister, but lesser than a mere candidate, K'thomi dog!" he laughed.

The Queen's eyes flickered over the frozen giant, and he came to life, bellowing.

Sarkond swept the rows of elders and their quiet amusement stung his pride. His green eyes flamed with malevolence.

"I shall show you magic, my Lords!"

His hand pointed suddenly at Chandar.

"This criminal is my slave—mine to dispose of at my will, and not subject to your laws. Behold, how I envelop him with a magic flame!"

He hissed uncouth words in a tongue unknown to Chandar. A yellow haze of flames flickered up about his booted feet. Chandar tried to leap out of the circle of flame, but was held within it as if by invisible walls. The eyes of the Enchanter flamed into his, with a devilish mockery. The K'thomi's voice whispered, so low that only Chandar could hear: "Your long road ends here, slime of Orm. Your tongue shall not betray me, for charred and blackened in the flames—"

The Queen rose to her feet.

"Cease, child of K'thom!"

Sarkond's laughter rose above the murmur of the sages.

She extended one imperious white hand and the dim hall filled with an immense and soundless flash of white light. The flames that narrowed around Chandar vanished utterly, upon the instant. And Sarkond cried out,—twisted suddenly, and snatched his cloak open. About his waist, his girdle of magical implements had become a *writhing serpent!*

He tore it loose with shaking hands, and flung it upon the tiles. The torpid reptile coiled slowly. With face pale as death and eyes that flamed with malignancy, the Enchanter said:

"You are pleased to play with me, Lady. Return my girdle to me, if you will. I apologize for my rashness."

Her laughter rang out, touched with malicious music.

"Ah, no, K'thomi, you might be tempted to return the jest. No, we shall let your girdle sleep here in the sunlight for awhile."

He measured her with appraising eyes.

"What is your intent, then?"

Llys smiled, her eyes dancing to Chandar. "Your wish to see the Flame was what brought you to the Land of Magic, was it not?"

He nodded, warily.

"Then I shall grant your wish."

Chandar started.

"Llys—no! Do not trust—"

She smiled sweetly at the Enchanter.

"If you still experience the same desire, I shall satisfy it. You shall see—the Flame!"

The Enchanter glanced around, licking his thin lips.

"You—are not jesting? You will truly grant my desire?"

Llys beckoned.

"I shall! Come—all of you—and the girl as well—you shall all behold the secret of the Flame—and then we shall know the truth!"

Bram's eyes were disturbed, angry. Sarkond's gleamed with relish and triumph. But Chandar read in Mnadis' eyes another emotion—one even stranger.

They left the Hall of Mages together.

To see—what?

9 DESCENT INTO THE ABYSS

THEY WENT through a small door that led to a staircase. At the head of the stair, Llys raised her jeweled sceptre in a peculiar sign. The slim metal wand glowed suddenly with a clear luminance the color and intensity of sunlight. Beside Chandar, the burly red-beard muttered sourly: "More magic! There has been nothing but sorcery from the day Kralian caught us off the Bay of Nephelis. Watch yourself, lad!"

"What?"

Bram slid his eyes from the golden figure of Mnadis, to the slim form of Llys in her robes of white silk-stuff.

"Two witches," he whispered hoarsely, "And both with eyes on you—and hearts as well, perhaps. When they discover they cannot get what they want—you watch out. We'll see magic, then!"

Chandar flushed beneath his tan.

"You're imagining things, old bear!"

Bram regarded him with a grin.

"I'm not imagining, lad. I see it in the lass's eye when she looks your way. Oh, she's a proud one, that girl,—proud. She thinks there's more between you and the golden witch than there is. She'd rather die, I say, than let you know what's in her heart—"

Ahead of them, the silvery peal of Llys' voice cut Bram's ramblings to silence.

"Silent now, and be careful, all of you. These stairs are steep."

They were descending a slowly winding stair, cut from the same glassy substance that all of Iophar seemed constructed from. The stairway was a sloping spiral, jutting from the wall of a great well or shaft which sank deep into the heart of the world. Dark it was, and chill . . . a penetrating cold moisture rose out of the black pit, making Mnadis shiver and draw her cloak more closely about her slim body. Only the clear magical light that the Queen bore illuminated this vast hole through the planet.

They went down—and down. Soon Mnadis was stumbling with weariness. But Sarkond seemed not to feel the touch of fatigue—an icy fire gleamed in his snake eyes. He was to discover *The Flame!*

They rested a time, and then went on, Llys leading, with Meliander behind her, followed by Chandar, Bram and the two K'thomi. The stairway seemed endless . . . the immense shaft seemed to be drilled all the way to the secret

heart of Iridar itself. Chandar tried to imagine what stupendous force or engine could possibly have hollowed out
this giant tube, but his imagination failed before the effort.
No, it could not have been the work of mere men. No
engineering marvel in all the lands he knew could compare
with this . . . not the great Cylinders of Psamathis, the
tower tombs where lie buried the age old Kings whose
entire reigns had been devoted to the task of raising their
own memorials . . . nor the vast and ancient Wall of Gol-
zunda, those vine-grown, jungle-buried ruins deep in the
Southlands, where some unknown and unmemoried race
of Jungle Lords had raised a man-made mountainridge of
stone beside the shore of the Peloma . . . nor the towering ramparts and splendid palaces of Heptapolis itself, the
Crown-City of the world . . . not all of these architectural
feats together could equal the gigantic task of emptying
this mighty shaft deep into the bowels of the planet. It
would take the strength of a God to perform this task
. . . the vast hand of some being as far beyond man's
little strength as man was above the reptiles.

But at last their dizzying descent into the abyss was
ended, and they stood before a door of some unknown
scarlet metal, seven times the height of a man. They rested
there for a moment, recovering their breath and allowing
the tiredness to seep out of their weary leg-muscles.

Chandar brushed drops of sweat from his brow with a
brawny forearm, and caught a glance from Llys. Her pure
soft eyes flashed with an unaccustomed glint of mockery,
deep in their pellucid azure depths.

"Tired, Prince?" she asked, the faintest echo of laughter
ringing behind her words.

"Yes, Lady," he said, frankly.

She made no reply, but the dimmest trace of a smile
flickered across her warm lips. *Now, by the Axe!* Chandar thought *I'll wager there is another—and easier—way
down this hole! She did this deliberately—the cat!* He
grinned at the thought.

"Look, lad!"

Bram clutched his shoulder, pointing. Cut into the weird
scarlet metal of the giant door was an emblem . . . a white
symbol of a flame, oval, pointed, dancing . . . the same

as the one Chandar and Bram had seen days earlier on the old parchment sea-chart in the Enchanter's cabin.

"The Flame . . ."

As if Chandar's whispered exclamation was a magical Word of Power, the vast leaves of the door swung inward silently, ponderously, their noiseless motion sending a chill of premonition through the Prince.

"Enter," Llys bade them.

They went through the vast open portal . . . and entered into a gigantic crystal fairyland! The walls and domed roof were of glittering glass, faceted and rough. From the dim vaulted ceiling, great crystal spears hung downward . . . weird and wonderfully beautiful was this cavern, like the enchanted dwelling place of some mysterious Spirit or Power in an old myth.

They gazed around at the glittering wonderland. Chandar was watchful. Bram gaped, open-mouthed in awe. Mnadis' face was closed . . . only her eyes glinted alertly, hiding some inner secret, as she observed—weighed—

Sarkond's voice was harsh, strident: "What is this place, my Lady?"

Llys answered him in cool, ringing words.

"It is where you wanted to be, Enchanter . . . where the truth of your words will be judged . . . the palace of The Flame."

Her voice echoed and reechoed through the dim vaulted cavern, drawing shivery glassy music from the long, dangling crystal spears which hung from the roof far above like some gigantic forest of icicles.

"Look!" Bram gasped.

Far above them somewhere among the confusion of planes and reflections, a dim light hovered, dancing, growing. It drew shimmering fire from a thousand angles and prisms of crystal as it descended, and the huddled figures watched it in silence and wonder.

It was a flame, a dancing oval of pure white light, that trembled and wavered in constant motion. Within its heart a slim core of intense utter light blazed, dazzling their eyes. Tall it was, taller than a grown man . . . but not of substance, thin and vaporous . . . a flickering spindle shape of immaterial light, fragile, slim. It descended slowly, casting a pure radiance upon their up-turned faces. Somehow, for all its fragility and elegance, they sensed an inner heart of terrific power held leased and quivering . . . the atomic force that sleeps, bound and chained, in the center of the stars. It cast a breath of cold awe across their hearts. They felt—all of them—puny and small before this slim oval white flame that danced before them.

It spoke—

"I have seen you before, though you knew it not, but never until now have I cared to look into your hearts and see there the truths that are written for such as I to read. I am the Flame you have sought, Sarkond of K'thom. Ask of me what you will, and I will answer. And when you have done with your questions . . . then I will answer again, in a way that is my own!"

The Enchanter gazed as one blinded, dazzled. Words hung on his thin lips, but he could not speak them. He stared in silence at the thing as it danced and wavered before him, a flickering spindle of light, as tall as a man. Within its vaporous lace of light . . . wrapped in the misty froth of curdled opalescence, the narrow core of blinding glory burned with supernatural fires.

"What—are—you?" he gasped.

The Flame answered again, its weird voice an inhuman piping music, soft as a whisper but clear as a bell of glass.

"I am The Flame. I am an intelligent entity of pure force, a living thing even as you are, save that the spark of life within you is hung about with walls of flesh and served with physical organs and fed with meat. I am pure Life, unhampered by flesh . . . free and eternal, indestructible. I drink the wine of life directly from the energy of my parent, the Sun, whereas you derive yours after the way of the beast, by the flesh of animals who have devoured the growing plants who have themselves imbibed of the energies of light. Within my structure, this process is simplified, and I drink the strength that sustains me directly from the Sun."

Sarkond gasped: "Child of—the Sun?"

The Flame danced, almost as if nodding. Its shrill, tinkling voice rose among the echoes.

"I was born in that hour when the Great Sun gave birth to the planets of this system. From the stupendous gouts of energy given off in that cataclysmic moment, came—I! I am older than the planets by a million years . . . for when they were slowly condensing from the Sun-stuff, I lived! I am a structure of pure force, and within me the alignment of electrons, that is the source of the life energy that vitalizes the protein molecule, exists . . . and has existed from the moment of that Creation. Perhaps the fury and chaos of that great explosion, when the Sun my parent threw off the incandescent stuffs that eventually became your planets, forced the electrons into a new structure . . . or perhaps I had always existed, sleeping within the fires of the Sun . . . I do not know. But I—lived! I watched the planets being born . . . tiny Nelidar, nearest to the Sun . . . cloud-veiled Phondar . . . savage, jungled Mnendar with its one moon . . . this world of Iridar with its two circling companions . . . huge Shomdar beyond the belt of scattered worldlets . . . yellow Iamdar belted with its titanic ring . . . and the other, more remote worlds beyond! I saw them being born and watched their clouds of incandescent gas slowly condense over the passage of immeasureable ages, slowly hardening and cooling into globes of dead, steaming rock. Through a vast and name- less aeon of time I watched rude seas wash their shores . . . mountains rise and continents erode into soil. I ob- served when the first tiny cells came into being, and sensed within their flecks of jelly a spark of that same fire that burned so brightly within my core. Throughout the ages of the Universe I have watched while those jelly-flecks grew and changed and forced themselves to swim, to climb, then to walk and fly. I have waited while age upon age went past me into the great darkness of eternity, waiting while intelligence developed within those flecks of jelly which were my tiny brothers. This world of Iridar became my home, so that I could better and more closely observe the phenomenon of life as it emerged and evolved itself, higher, even higher towards—I! Someday your children's children's children ten thousand million generations in the unknown future will slough off the flesh and become

even as I, things of dancing light, intelligence of pure energy, eternal—deathless—all wise . . ."

10 THE JUDGMENT OF THE FLAME

THE THIN, fluting voice of the entity softened into a purr.

"I have watched your ancestors toil up the long and steep road from apehood to where you now stand. Millions of years it took you, and many millions more lie before you. Your children shall one day seek out and define the laws of nature, as the Philosophers of ancient Polaria did in ages gone, and learn the inner workings of those forces which you foolishly call magic, and which you blindly play with when you toy with those magical instruments which survived the Fall of that Kingdom. You, Sorceror of K'thom, the magic tools you place so much reliance upon, and your limited mastery of them which you foolishly call your "wisdom," you do but fumble with the toys left behind when Polaria went down beneath my wrath! I slew those Philosophers because they ignorantly tampered with the forces that held this planet in her place; I whelmed that land beneath a million tons of snow and ice for their folly . . . and those few instruments that survived the Fall became the foundations of your science of magic. Ah, no matter . . . someday your descendants will duplicate the mighty workshops of Lost Polaria, but this time they will investigate the secrets of nature with more care . . . they will reach out for the stars and they shall take them, and your children a billion generations it may be from now, will walk the lush ways of that Third Planet, Mnendar, planting the seeds of men in a first tiny outpost that shall someday outlive the planet of their birth. But that is for the future. For the present . . . ah, children, I see into your hearts! I read the neuron patterns of your minds as you can glance into an open book. I know you, Bram of Orm . . ."

The red-beard flinched, and the voice of The Flame
rose strong and warm:

*"I see the strength of you, and the courage, and the loy-
alty. I saw all that when I observed your broken body
hanging in the Wall of Ice, slain by K'thomi magic. I
brought your spirit back from the Great Sleep that lies
beyond life, yes, and I healed your terrible wounds and
breathed the breath of life back into your flesh! All this
I did—I!—because I see the unselfish love within you, and
the devotion toward the tall youth by your side. Fear me
not, Bram of Orm, for your life shall be long and good,
with much service in it, and with much fighting in it, for
that is what you love most, next to your Prince."*

The invisible gaze of the Flame seemed next to shift to
Chandar. His skin prickled from that weird surveillance.

*"And I know you, Chandar of Orm! From of old I have
guarded and nourished your House, for from its seed and
from your blood a mighty race of Kings shall arise, into
whose hands I give sovereignty over all the lands and seas
of Iridar. You and your children, and your children's
children shall create a powerful and an enlightened Realm
that shall serve my ends, unite the scattered and warring
princedoms of this barbaric age, and lay the foundations
of the future. That Axe by your side I delivered into the
hands of your ancestors, and my will locked powers within
its very fabric and substance . . . forces which only those
of your blood can unleash. Guard it well, Chandar of
Orm, for it is one of the Three Arch-Talismans of this
world, as you know. Your children shall search for the
Second, the Sword of Psamathis, in good time, for it is
important that all three of these sigils be in your posses-
sion, for the safety of your House. As for the Third Arch-
Talisman, it may have been lost in the foundering of the
Polarian continent. No one knows."*

Chadar felt Llys looking at him, and turned to meet her
candid eyes. Was it an apology that hovered in her gaze?
Was it a . . . promise? He stared back, smiling gently.

The searching gaze of The Flame fell at last on Sarkond.
Under its pressure, the gaunt Enchanter of K'thom drew
himself up, lips sealed, eyes blazing with lambent green
fires.

"And you, Sarkond of K'thom," The Flame said softly, "I know you, as well. You sought with subtle lies and false demeanor to befool the Mages of Iophar and seek out the secret of The Flame. You knew that the power behind The Flame lends tremendous strength to anyone who possesses it, and you would learn that power and use it for your own ends. I read your heart, and I see lies and deceit, greed and avarice, and a black lust for Kingship that eats at the roots of your soul like a great canker of decay. You would use your magic to carve out upon the helpless surface of Iridar a great Empire of blood and iron and agony. You would use that power to enchain the bodies and the hearts and the minds of all men, so that you should be exalted above them. I knew of your coming long before you were near, and it is within my power to grant your wish. What say you, Wizard of the Southlands . . . shall I grant your wish?"

Consternation awoke. Llys reached out, grasping one hand on Chandar's shoulder and stretching the other in appeal towards the hovering, dancing spindle of glory.

"Lord—no!"

The Flame silenced her calmly.

"Quiet, child. Let us hear the K'thomi speak. Well, Sarkond of K'thom, what say you?"

"I—" Sarkond faltered, his voice failing. He groped for words, a flush of triumph rising in his sallow cheeks.

"Lord—Great One! Give me power, and I shall exalt you above all Gods who have ever reigned since time began! I shall build an Empire in your name, you read my mind truly, I would create an Empire—but it shall worship you, God of the Flame! Give me your power—stretch out your hand to me—power and glory shall be yours, above all Gods!" he gasped out, stammering.

Serenely The Flame said: *"There are no Gods, save in man's dreams. Will you exalt me, truly, Wizard?"*

"Yea, truly, Lord!"

"And shall I exalt you, Enchanter of K'thom, above all men? It is within my power to do so if I wish."

For all his tension, Chandar felt a faint echo of mockery rang in the voice of The Flame . . . like a cat playing with a mouse. He closed his hand over Llys'—and watched for the end of this strange game.

Sarkond gasped, "Yes, Lord, exalt me!"

The Flame rang out like silver trumpets calling:

"Then behold, the judgement of The Flame!"

A net of sparkling white fire fell upon the rapt K'thomi, threading about his gaunt limbs with tendrils of living flame. He screamed—beating frantically at the web as it closed about him. The stench of burning flesh entered their nostrils like a blow. The dull green robes of the Enchanter blackened and burst into fire.

The high silver laughter of The Flame rose above the noise, detached, remote, God-like.

An unseen force, like an invisible hand, plucked the burning corpse from the ground and hurled it high above their heads, spinning in the dim darkness of the vaulted ceiling of the great cavern. Reflections of the fires glittered in the crystal prisms. Sarkond was a blazing hieroglyphic, written on the darkness.

"Behold the justice of The Flame; Sarkond of K'thom is exalted far above your heads, you children of men, but not as he would have wished. So perish all who seek knowledge only to serve their selfish greed!"

As a candle snuffed out by a giant hand, the flaming figure vanished in the darkness. The Enchanter was dead.

Chandar relaxed, sliding his arm about the slim waist of Llys. By his side, stout old Bram let out an explosive breath in a whistle of sheer relief.

"Ah, lad,—lad! That was a close one; there for a time I feared the yellow snake would win his way after all!"

The Flame said serenely, *"My justice is not yours, Bram of Orm. But we serve the same ends, you and I."*

And then the ice-cold voice of Mnadis cut across the scene.

"And what of me, Flame? Have you read my heart as well?"

They had all forgotten the silent girl, huddled against the door apart from them. Startled, they turned, to see that now Mnadis stood clear, feet set wide apart and hands on richly curved hips. An air of heady insolence hovered about her, glittering in the mocking gaze of slitted eyes and laughing in the smiling curve of her ripe lips. Brazen, she stood forth like a slim golden statue—against the blazing glory of The Flame!

"Do you know all, Flame,—truly all? Do you know, then, that you are not alone in this Universe, that there are others like you, Beings of Power, Entities of Pure Force? Others—one, at least, a Flame of Evil and Darkness?"

Puzzled, halting, The Flame said: *"A—Dark—Flame?"*

She laughed, a golden torrent of malicious sound.

"Aye! A Dark Flame—and I am its servant and priest-ess, even as yon milk-white maiden is yours. Ah, Flame, you could not know, any more than these poor mortals!"

Her laughing eyes blazed at Chandar.

"That fool there thought I loved him! And all the time I but played with him, seeking to learn the secret of the Axe! And that other fool, whom you snuffed out as a man might crush an insect, that fool who thought he was my master! Ah, there is a jest for the very Gods—he lorded it over me, and all those years I possessed a power so far beyond his that it makes me almost your equal, White Flame!"

"What—power?" The Flame inquired.

"This."

She whipped loose her hair and it fell in a foaming scar-let-golden mane about her shoulders. From its tangled depths she drew out a Jewel . . . a sparkling crystal no larger than a fingernail.

It glittered like a nugget of ice in the soft palm of her hand, its facets radiating needles of ice-cold light into their astonished eyes.

She laughed again—triumphantly!

"Look upon it well, Flame, you who are so omnipotent! Gaze deeply into it, with those senses of yours that can read like a parchment scroll the hearts and minds of men —those senses that can dispel the mists that hide the future from the present, and that open the locked secrets of all space and time to your divine sight! Look upon this gem and tell me one thing—one little thing—out of your Godlike wisdom. Do you know what it is?"

Before The Flame could speak, Mnadis tossed back her

burning tide of hair and laughed again, her slim throat
a singing golden curve of terrible beauty.

"It is the Third Talisman, Flame! The Lost Talisman
of Polaria—overwhelmed, so you in all your wisdom
thought and believed, overwhelmed and buried far below
the ice and snows that hide the Lost Land from man's
knowledge. Ah, but you are not so wise, Flame of Iophar!
The Dark Flame is wiser far, than you! Wiser, yes, and
stronger too. For where you would waste your powers
striving to build puny humanity into star-conquerors, the
Dark Flame seeks to destroy! To gain mastery over this
Universe—to hurl sun upon sun, to sweep the stars together into a vast cataclysm—to send the far galaxies of
space thundering together and bring all of creation down
in ruin—and then to build a new Universe after his own
design, a Universe in which he is supreme! Is that not a
Godlike ambition, O mighty Flame of White?"

Her torrent of fierce eloquence held them all frozen,
aghast with amazement. She laughed again, and brandished
the glittering Jewel of Polaria above her head.

"Yes, the Dark Flame sent his agents into Polaria ages
ago, and stole the Arch-Talisman long before you over-
came the doomed land with your mountains of ice. Shielded from your gaze by a power as great as yours, it has
served the Dark Flame all this time. When my Master
learned that Sarkond of K'thom would seek out The Flame
of Iophar, he gave the Jewel into my hands and I became
Sarkond's accomplice, although all the while he knew not
that I was greater than he, who served no mightier master
than his own greed.

"And so I have sought out you in your hidden place,
White Flame, and can tell my Master of your powers, which
are no greater than his, and of your age, which is no older
than his. And now he can unleash his forces against this
little world of Iridar, knowing at last your full strength, for
doubt of you has held him back all these aeons. Farewell,
and when the shadows of the Dark Flame blacken your
shining skies—then shall you know the power of the Dark
Flame!"

A fume of weird black radiance poured from the Jewel
of Polaria, enveloping the slim golden Mnadis as within a

fog. Her triumphant laughter rang out sharp and clear above the dim thunder of the mysterious force.

Llys screamed, and Chandar steadied her, sliding one brown arm about her soft shoulders. By his side, Bram cursed steadily.

"I never trusted that witch from the first moment I saw her cold eyes! I knew, deep down, that she was as treacherous in her own way as that yellow snake, the old K'thomi who lived and died thinking he was her master. Damn it all, lad, what's she doing now?"

The weird black light swelled about her in a dark cloud. A breath of icy wind came from it. Within the sphere of darkness her golden limbs could be glimpsed, as flashes through a cloud of ebon vapor.

Even as they watched, the surface of the sphere seemed to harden, to crystallize—for a moment it glittered before them, a perfect ball of polished black crystal, reflecting their astonished faces in distorted curves, as in a flawed or warped mirror—and then, suddenly, the black sphere moved, hurling against the ponderous doors of scarlet metal, which gave way before it as if they were made of a substance no stronger than mere paper.

Out into the titanic shaft the sphere of darkness moved, vanishing from their sight.

Mnadis was—gone.

11 THE AXE OF ORM

THUNDER smote the crystal walls, as the great doors of scarlet metal were rent, reverberating from plane to plane and drawing a weird, clashing music from the forest of glass spears that dangled from the dim vault, among whose shadowy vastnesses the echoes became remote and faded into silence.

Into a long silence.

Bram, Chandar and Llys stared emptily at each other.

Lord Meliander pondered gravely, combing his long beard
with slow fingers. The Flame hovered and danced above
them, its fires dimmed and muted.

Then Llys lifted her slim white arms.

"What shall we do, Lord?" she whispered, appealingly.
The Flame brooded.

*"For ages I have wondered if there were another such
as I within the reaches of this Universe, or if I were the
only Child of the Sun . . . a lonely orphan amid the star
spaces. Now that this revelation has come, I doubt . . .
I doubt . . ."*

Chandar roused himself.

"What do you doubt, Lord?"

*"If this Dark Flame, my brother, is not . . . stronger
. . . than myself."* Its fires brightened, veils of pearly
lace unfolding from the incandescent glory of its blazing
core. *"Do you hear, mortal? I doubt—I, who have moved
like an immortal God down the aeons of time, my authority
unquestioned, my power unchallenged! Proud was I of my
parenthood, of my uniqueness and my wisdom. And now
there is another such as I, sharing my dominion . . .
and that other, who could have been my friend—is my
enemy! My enemy and the enemy of all life, and of that
puny race that I would raise through ages of slow and
painful growth, to a position close to my own height."*

"What shall we do?"

It was Meliander who spoke, and the high silvery voice
of The Flame crashed out like a bright trumpet-call.

"We shall fight, mortals, fight together, you and I!"

"How can we fight . . . one like unto yourself?" Llys
asked, and the glittering voice laughed.

*"You shall see, Maid of Iophar! You shall see powers
unleashed which this world has not known since the far
time when I seared this mighty cavern out of the rock with
my lightnings. But we must work swiftly. The Witch of
K'thom, who is the minister of the Dark Flame, will return
to Shiangkor where she shall awaken or summon into being my dark brother. We must be there."*

"But Shiangkor is many, many hours distant, even by
the enchanted flying ship of Sarkond," Chandar said.

The Flame said: *"My powers shall carry you there far*

*swifter than a ship of magic! Trust to me, child, and you
shall traverse Jalangir Val, the Great Sea, as swift as the
winds of heaven."*

"I shall trust in you, and do your bidding," Chandar
said. The blade of the Axe flashed in the dancing light.

*"Swiftly, then! I shall transport the lot of you to Shiang-
kor, where you must seek out and destroy the Red Witch
who bears the lost Arch-Talisman. It will take her time,
precious time, to summon her Master."*

"And you, Lord? Will you not be with us?"

*"In good time, Chandar of Orm, in good time. I shall
come if she summons the Dark Flame, for while you have
power in the Axe of your House to slay the Dark Flame's
mortal minister, only I can challenge the Dark One in his
power! Now go, and work swiftly!"*

A mist of lacy light sprang from The Flame to envelop
them. Llys shrank within the strong circle of Chandar's
brawny arm; Meliander remained calm; Bram grumbled
but did not stir. The veil of light folded about them, cradled
them within a fragile-seeming sphere of light—and lifted—

Up the enormous length of the great pit they soared,
with the air shrieking around them. Although they moved
at terrific speed, they felt no physical effect of it. It was
as if they stood in a stationary room, watching a moving
picture rush past. Up they went, and up, and then—slowing their speed, they floated out into the great Hall of Wizards, empty now of its council, where the enchanted girdle
of dead Sarkond still lay in torpid coils in a pool of sunlight.

The glowing sphere of light drifted out between the
enormous pillars and then ascended straight up. The glassy
spires and glittering domes of Iophar shrank beneath them
into a tiny spark of color, surrounded by the dull green
and brown patchwork of the Land of Magic.

At this enormous height, taller than any mountain on
the planet of Iridar, they gazed down at the whole Kingdom
spread out beneath them as upon a painted chart. The
faint white circle of the Wall of Ice traced an arc of milky
foam against the dim blue waters of Jalangir Val the Great
Sea. The Wall itself was invisible from this height, but the
foamline where the waves of the sea beat and broke against
the ice-barrier, formed a creamy circle of whiteness, clearly

visible from this great height. Far to the north a smudge of black smoke, where the magic Wall of Fire burned eternally, showed faintly against the dull landscape-colors. They could dimly make out the far green forests of seacoast Shombia to the northwest, and from this height the twin moons showed—not as crescents or blank discs of light, but as rounded orbs.

Then the sphere shot into motion. League upon blue league of sea flashed past far beneath them. The blazing disc of the sun, reflected in the ocean beneath them, seemed to race with them.

Faster than the Enchanter's galley of *seraeli*-wood, they hurtled through the skies of Iridar. Swifter than the winged crimson dragons of Iophar, they flashed through space. With the speed of thought itself they neared the shores of Shiangkor. The dim outline of the Hundred Isles became visible . . . and the arched curve of land that was the Bay of Nephelis entered their vision, where long before Chandar and Bram had been taken by Admiral Kralian.

They approached the city of Shiangkor, descending through the shrieking air. It swam up towards them, a glittering dot that unfolded with the swiftness of a magic vision. They saw the steep cliffs, and clinging to their heights, the great towers and walls of rough yellow stone. Slim towers crowned with peaked roofs of dark red tile swam into sight, and narrow cobbled streets where market throngs turned a thousand pale faces skyward to watch the descent of the flying ball of white luminance. They could see the long quays and docks, where slim naval ships of war and fat-hulled merchant galleys rode at anchor in the choppy water, the level rays of the low-hanging afternoon sun touching their vast sails to scarlet.

The sphere drifted over the city of Shiangkor, weaving with dreamlike ease between the tall towers. Then the great King's Hall loomed before them, its frowning bastions rich with the banners of Niamnon, scarlet and green and black. The sphere floated into a great window.

They were in the great audience hall, crowded with brightly clothed nobles and copper-mailed guards. Down from the vaulted roof the sphere floated, landing on the checkered pave as lightly as a drifting fleck of down. The courtiers shrank from it, murmuring and gasping with consternation.

When the sphere touched the pave, it flashed out of existence. Bram, Chander, Llys and Meliander stood in the middle of the hall.

Niamnon sat enthroned upon his dais, seated in the great chair that had been carved from a single tusk of a sea dragon. His shimmering robes glittered in the flaring torch light, that caught jeweled fire from his gauds and ornaments. Although his heavy face was pale against the bristling black beard, his jaw was firmly set and his cold black eyes were wary. The Winged Dragon upon his brows caught the torch light in fiery sparkles.

Guards had closed around Chandar and the others, but the King waved them back, allowing the four to approach the throne. He stared—and laughed!

"Now, by all the Seven Gods! It is the wolf cub of Orm, come to visit me! By Zantain, King of the Gods, I had not dreamt it might be you, dropping from the clouds like a wizard. Well, you must have liked our hospitality before, to visit us again so soon . . . indeed, I have been busy thinking up ways to—shall I say?—entertain you, did you ever chance within my borders again." The King laughed gustily, but his mirth was not echoed by the court nobles, who stirred uneasily, gazing at the four strangers.

Chandar spoke swiftly: "Listen to me, Niamnon, time enough for you and I to settle our differences later. We are here on an urgent mission—"

The King leaned back in his throne, smiling lazily and toying with a rope of jewels.

"Indeed! Say on, stripling."

"Mnadis of K'thom, the servant of Sarkond, has returned —so we believe—to the city. She must be found, and swiftly—"

"Aye, I remember the wench well. She vanished when my Enchanter left, and you and the burly red bear at your side were gone in the same hour. I have long wondered who rescued who—and why—"

"No time for that now! You must send your guards out to search the city for her. She must be found!"

The King smiled again.

"Ah, yes . . . and is there anything else you want, Prince of Orm? Would you like a banquet served for you and your friends? Perhaps you would care for a visit to the palace treasury, to pick out some gems for that wench beside you? You have but to speak, O Prince! We are all your servants!"

At that, the courtiers tittered, recovering some of their presence of mind. The grim line of guards relaxed, chuckling. Llys blushed scarlet, and veiled her eyes.

"Niamnon, I do not jest! This is important! I can explain—"

The King dropped his smiling mask.

"Nor am I jesting, spittle! I know not what wild hope you are working towards, but I have you now, and you shall serve my pleasure here!" His fleshy face moved in a sneer.

"The arena still waits for you, and shall soon enjoy your presence . . . as I shall enjoy watching your death."

Chandar's eyes flashed.

"We are wasting time, King. I was a fool to think you might listen—"

He sprang forward towards the throne, the Axe of Orm flashing into his hand. A guard stepped out—Chandar felled him with a single stroke, and felled another—splitting his face in two bloody halves like a great ripe fruit. He stood alone on the lower step of the dais.

"Well, King—shall I come up to you, or will you come down to me?" he asked impatiently.

The King sprang to his feet.

"Since you are in such a hurry to die—let it be now!" he hissed. His eyes flicked to the Captain of the Guard. "Gorse! Your blade!"

The Captain's sword hissed from its leathern scabbard. He tossed it flashing across the space between them, and Niamnon snapped it from mid-air in one brawny fist. He stood on the top step of the dais, flickering it in a whistling arc about his head—then sprang like a savage *kreagar* straight upon Chandar.

The youth had been watching, wary against such a move, and the great Axe crashed against the blade, bringing the King to his knees.

He sprang erect, snarling. The blade flicked out—*klang!*
—meeting the Axe again.

They descended to the paved floor, which emptied of
people, making room for them. For a long moment they
circled like suspicious cats, then Chandar flashed the Axe.
It rang against Niamnon's blade but did not break it. The
King laughed and closed in. His agile sword wove a glittering net about Chandar, forcing him back against a pillar.

Llys put her hands to her mouth.

The Axe struck out, singing. The sword screeched, spitting sparks. Niamnon took a vicious back-handed swipe at
Chandar's head, but the Prince ducked. The blade rang
like a gong against the pillar and tinkled to the pave, falling
from Niamnon's nerveless hand.

With a hoarse cry, the King sprang backwards, lifting an
arm against the expected blow . . . but Chandar merely
stood, leaning upon the Axe, watching him with an amused
grin. He beckoned with an open hand.

"Go, King, pick up your blade again. Don't be afraid."

Bram bellowed with laughter, but the guards and courtiers stood in a strained silence. Niamnon glared around
him, his face working, flushed with fury.

He snatched the sword from the floor and came at
Chandar in a wild, slashing attack, snarling and spitting
with rage. Chandar easily countered every blow, holding
the Axe before his chest, deflecting each stroke with a deft
twist of his wrist.

The King staggered backward, panting and scarlet from
the unfamiliar exertion. His chest heaved beneath the heavy
robes and silks.

Chandar laughed, boyishly.

"Come, come, King of Shiangkor! Don't stop now—you
have yet to kill me."

Niamnon's mouth worked, chewing his lips. He ripped
away the jeweled sleeves of the gown and bared his heaving chest. Then he came at Chandar again, blade flashing
furiously, casting sparks.

"Lad! We are losing time!" Bram called. "The wench
will be raising her demon god!"

Chandar turned his head at Bram's shout, and in that
split second the darting sword flashed past his guard and

thudded with its flat against his temple. His vision blurred
and he sagged to his knees.

The King roared with laughter, and hurled the point
straight for his heart—

The Orm-Axe woke!

A quivering forked flame sprang from it to the hurtling
sword—a soundless flash of white light. Niamnon screamed
and staggered back from the electric shock. Chandar got
to his feet, shaking his head numbly to gather his sluggish
senses together.

The King sprang forward again, sword raised over his
head, swinging downward in a mighty stroke. Chandar
raised the Axe, bracing it with both arms, his tough muscles
rippling with tension.

The sword—broke.

It snapped off short at the hilt, the severed blade ringing
against the pave a dozen feet away. Niamnon turned and
ran.

"Gorse!" he screamed—"Kill him!"

The burly guardsman lifted his javelin, sighting along
the shaft, but the Axe of Orm was alive with power. The
forces that had slumbered in it for generations were loosed.

It spat a bolt of wriggling fire that snapped in a dazzling
arc from Axe-blade to spear-point. Gorse shrieked, whirled
in a sudden cloud of flames. Other guards sprang forward.
Chandar turned the Axe against them. They blackened—
withered—died. Then the guards broke and ran, followed
by the screaming horde of courtiers who fought desperately to escape this lightning wielding Nemesis.

The crackle and hum of power died. The Axe quivered
in Chandar's hand.

Against a far pillar, the King crouched, his pallid face
a quivering, sweat-glistening mask of terror.

"Don't kill me! Don't!" he shrieked as Chandar slowly
advanced on him. "I shall repair the wrongs I did to you!
I'll pay you—anything—"

"Can you repay a father, burned alive?" Chandar asked
softly. "Or a family butchered by stealth and treachery?"

He flung his head back, tossing loose his black mane,
thundering forth the ancient war-cry of his people.

"Harah—Ormsgard!" Chandar roared, and clove Niamnon to the brain.

The last King of Shiangkor toppled forward, face down, into a pool of blood.

The empty Crown rolled across the pave.

Chandar crushed it beneath his heel.

12 BATTLE OF THE GODS

THEY CAME across the hall to him. Llys nestled softly in his arms and he could feel the wetness of her tear-stained cheek against his shoulder, where a blade slash left it bare. Bram thumped his back.

"Lad—lad! It made me proud to see you," he crowed. "That was a duel that the bards of Orm shall sing of for a thousand years! If old Ganelon were here to see it, he'd weave a saga from the tale."

Even Meliander was moved. He smiled, gravely.

"Well done, my Prince, well done. Although Niamnon's blood is my own, he richly deserved such a death—I am proud of you."

Llys raised her face towards him, lips parted.

And then the sun went out.

A great shadow choked the hall, dimming the flaring torches that burnt along the walls in bronze sconces.

Bram snatched up a fallen sword. "More magic!" he rumbled.

"Mnadis!" Chandar exclaimed. "While we fooled around here, she has raised her devil-master!"

Meliander nodded.

"We must find her quickly—stop her, before it is too late—unless perchance it already be too late."

"I'll find her," Bram growled. "And wet this dry steel in her witch's blood!"

"Come on!" Chandar called, running across the great room towards a distant door.

They emerged on a height above the city. Shiangkor lay, meshed in webs of darkness. The sunset sky was visibly darkening. The wings of blackness swept above them, faster than clouds. The towers merged with the cloak of shadows. They could hear the cries and calls of citizens, desperate, frightened, stumbling about in the night-thick blackness. Chandar grasped Llys' hand.

"Are we all here? Bram? Where's Bram?"

"Look!" Llys' slim hand was a faint white blur in the choking shadow. Chandar strained his eyes, to see what she had noticed . . .

Then he saw.

Above them, high in the vault of the heavens, a Black Flame burned.

Darker even than the darkness . . . a crawling blot of clotted ebon against the shadow-veiled sky, it hovered. Black it was, and black . . . deeper and darker than the unlighted abyss between the suns . . . the utter nadir of darkness, black as the soundless, lightless vacuum of outer space itself.

The Dark Flame.

It danced and flickered against the shadow sky, a dance of triumph, a dance of final victory. And as it danced, it grew . . . gathering its strength . . . growing larger, darker, eclipsing the heavens, shadowing the twin moons of Iridar.

And from the Dark Flame, as from the dark sphere that had invaded the golden body of Mnadis, came the coldness of deep space. The chill breath of the winds that blow between the worlds—touched them.

Cold . . . colder than any winter wind . . . colder than the hyperborean snows of the great ice-cap, or the million tons of solid ice that overwhelmed and buried Polaris. The deathly cold of space itself. A cold that blasted, searing the flesh like a flame of darkness.

Below them, in the midnight ways of the city, people screamed, despairingly. Into Chandar's racing mind came a vague strain from the old bardic myths, the songs of the future Twilight Days, when the Gods would die and the planet Iridar grow old and parched . . . a thread of song from the old, prophetic epics . . .

Black shadow, night of Gods,
Cold the touch of Drega's kiss,
Like the wind from the Abyss.
Dark the world the Demon treads,
Neath his dragon-winged car,
On the field the Gods are dead,
Dead the world of Iridar . . .

He shivered in the biting chill, shaking off such haunted thoughts. Grimly he clutched the smooth handle of the Axe. Would its power be strong enough . . . ?

He raised it before his face, blade outwards, clasping one hand above and one hand beneath, holding it steady with iron hands.

"What are you going to do?" Meliander asked.

Chandar of Orm shook his head defiantly.

"I don't know. But I'll try anything—"

Desperately he wracked his mind, searching his memory for those uncouth sylables of power the Enchanter had taught him, there, on the deck of the black galley . . . the secret spell that unlocked the full power of the magic Orm-Axe . . . the cant that released the full tides of enormous energy, sealed within the stone and metal of the Arch-Talisman. How did it go?

To his mind came the scene. He could remember the livid face of the Sorceror, his burning eyes and gaunt, stooped form in the dull green robe . . . the thin, pale lips twisting like pallid worms, as they repeated to him the weird verse that was the Key . . .

He said it aloud, in a great ringing voice.

"Yuth-Kaathak ngom'm! Ygar naa Ithorthak!
Sh'ayaa Ubb nagarr'nya Ib! Ib-nya gryalak!"

The Axe—lit!

A flickering nimbus of pale flame grew about it. It trembled in his hands, like the muscles of a steed ready for the battle-charge. An electric thrill of power moved up his arm. His senses cleared—his eyes grew eagle-sharp. He drank the heady wine of power, laughing.

He seemed to grow in stature, till he towered over them.

Llys shrank back beside Meliander, her blue eyes wide.
Chandar laughed!

The flickering web of light grew—strengthened—beat
against the encroaching darkness with pulsing fires, casting
a blazing halo of radiant force about Chandar. Far below,
on the cobbled twisting streets, he could see the white faces
of the Shiangkori, upturned in awe and wonder. He laughed
again, tasting the power of the Gods.

The Axe burned brightly now, too bright for the eye to
endure. The blade was hidden at the center of a ball of
incandescence. Chandar leveled the flaming Axe at the
great scab of clotted darkness that hung to the sky.

Lightning flashed from the Axe! A great torrent of energy poured from its quivering blade, a writhing snake of
white fire that flashed up and struck the Dark Flame with
a blaze of fury.

The people cried out . . . but the Dark One seemed
unharmed. Seemed, in fact, to drink the lightning blast,
and from it, to grow even deeper, even darker, even larger.

Chandar hurled another crackling bolt of white force
—and another—and still another. The shadow-shrouded
sky was alive with white flame. Sizzling sparks dropped
along the stone parapet where he stood in the godlike
blaze of power, withering the climbing vines and marking
the stone with smears of black ash.

But the Dark Flame—grew.

Now a cold tide of remorseless force poured on the
Prince of Orm from above. His radiant halo faded—his
strength ebbed. He fought back, hurling a blinding torrent
of flame . . . but it thundered against a dark shield of
invisible force, and rebounded in a shower of pyrotechnics.

The Dark Flame was stronger than he.

Weakening, he sagged against the low stone railing.

The fires of the Axe—ebbed. Faded.

Beneath the pouring shower of cold and darkness, he
felt his senses swim—his vision blurred. But he fought
back desperately, doggedly, summoning strength for one
final great assault upon the Sun of Blackness that hovered
above Shiangkor, and above the whole world.

And then the whole city seemed to take a great breath
—a many-throated gasp. Llys cried: "Look!" All eyes

were fixed at something far above the city, above even the hovering Flame of Darkness—

A dancing wisp of delicate white flame flashed and blazed upon the breast of the nighted sky.

The attack on Chandar ceased abruptly. His knees buckled beneath him and he sank to the floor of the cold balcony, the Axe of Orm sagging from his strengthless hand.

The White Flame danced.

It seemed dwarfed against the great ball of blackness. A mere wisp of fragile light, flickering against the Black One. A breath could extinguish it as a blown candle flame . . . and yet it endured the icy blast of stellar wind that blew from the core of the Dark Flame.

And it grew, as if it too feeded upon its adversary's expended power. The frigid wind that blew from the Dark One—as remorselessly chill as the breath of the tomb, or the black winds that blow between the worlds—did not even make it waver. Gradually its lacy veils withdrew, and it blazed above the shadowed spires of Shiangkor in all its unearthly splendour.

A bolt of utter light sprang from the White Flame—but failed to penetrate the shield of darkness. Another—a great crackling, writhing serpent of electric fire that lit the nighted city with a soundless flare of energy!

The darkness—*winced.*

Another and another bolt of dazzling fire hammered against the clotted Blackness, like the fiery sledge of Nidir, Smith of the Gods! The Blackness withdrew, gathered in upon itself. To Chandar's dazed eye, the Dark One seemed boiling with inconceivable fury—a spinning nebula of complete darkness, a seething vortex of black force.

The Dark Flame struck. An arm of darkness enclosed the White Flame, like a curling tentacle of ebon mist. It closed about The Flame, dimming its fire—thickening—closing down. It was like a hand of black smoke, quenching a tiny lamp. Llys drew her breath and Meliander muttered prayers—prayers, or incantations, or perhaps both—under his breath.

The heavens burst open!

A blazing display of lightning shattered and dispersed

the arm of shadow—illuminating the sky with the fury of incandescent light. Thunder rolled and bellowed across the sky in peal after peal of deep-throated music.

For now the battle was joined in earnest. The heavens were transformed in mere moments into a cosmic battle-ground, where warring Gods were locked in stupendous combat. Bolts of livid white fury and thunderstrokes of ebon darkness crossed—collided—struck home! The wind arose and the very atmosphere was whipped into a frenzy. A screaming gale awoke above the city. The whole sky was alight now with flickering sheets of fire and scudding sheets of blackness. All was one vast howling storm of mingled light and darkness.

The towers shook beneath the raw, elemental fury of this titanic battle between the Gods. Chandar, still clinging nervelessly to the balcony, felt the solid stone quiver beneath him, to the gigantic concussions of the fantastic battle raging above. Now the White Flame and the Dark were locked together in one swirling cloud of intermingled fires. Bolts of black fury scorched the air with searing cold— blasts of dazzling flame seethed across the heavens, super-heating the air into boiling winds. Thunder shook the city to its granite-founded heart, the towers and temples of Shiangkor trembling to the erratic rhythms of the colliding Gods.

At the base of the cliffs, the raging winds whipped the black sea to frenzy. Great galleys swung and rocked— heavy cables snapped—the ships ground into one another with crushing force and dissolved into wreckage upon the foaming waves. A muted thunder came from the Street of Thieves, where rotten tenements collapsed in a landslide of brick and timber. Screams arose from the massed pop-ulace—they ran hither and thither through the thundering streets, bowed beneath the stupendous fury of the storm.

And then a sudden bolt of lightning lit the sky, and by its numbing light, they glimpsed a slim figure high above them, on the upper tiers of the building. A girl, her crimson hair a sanguine banner streaming against the fury of the wind, her flesh gleaming tawny in the crackling, intermittent light.

Mnadis, Red Witch of K'thom!

Through the mad chaos of whirling wind and fire, Chandar saw her stand, braced against the shocks of wind and thunder. She was laughing, her eyes blazing with the mad green fires. The mocking music of her wild mirth shrilled above the howling tempest. And in her hand the magic Jewel of Polaris blazed. An aura of weird black light vibrated from the Arch-Talisman, pouring its dark force into the chaotic sky.

Meliander clutched the Prince of Orm, pulling him to his feet. Chandar staggered dizzily, as the Wizard shouted above the bellowing waves of thunder.

"She is using the force of the Jewel against its creator! You must bring the Axe into play—throw its strength against the Dark Flame! Hurry!"

Weakly, Chandar shook his head. His strength was gone, he could use the Axe no more.

Above the thunder, he heard the silvery mocking peals of Mnadis' laughter. The black vibrations poured out in quivering waves of eerie force.

Chandar began gathering his strength. Taking a deep, long breath, he bent and caught up the fallen Axe. It weighed like sullen lead in his slack fingers.

And then the intermittent blaze of lightning revealed another figure clinging to the rooftop. A burly man with bull shoulders and blown mane of hair, cut like a silhouette of black paper against the blazing white fire.

Bram.

In a daze, Chandar suddenly realized that the red beard had parted from them there in the pall of swift darkness that had clouded the Hall. In the rush of events he had not thought of it till now. But obviously the bearded giant had gone seeking the Red Witch, knowing the swift shadow over the city was her witchcraft's work.

They watched, as the red-beard clambered slowly across the spired roof, coming up behind the girl. Waves of deafening thunder buffeted his bent shoulders. The shrieking winds clawed at him, tore at his arms, as if seeking to break his hold. But he came on.

Mnadis did not see him there behind her. She stood on the edge of the roof, legs spread and braced against the wings of the storm, both hands holding the darkly blazing

Jewel aloft. She was still laughing, her scarlet mane a tangled cloud tossed on the waves of thunder.

Like a great black spider, the burly Ormsling crept across the steep roof. Chandar's fascinated gaze caught the metallic twinkle of a blade clenched between Bram's teeth. Half of him wanted to cry out—to warn the slim, laughing girl—

She was still laughing when the foot-long blade slid between her shoulders.

She faltered—and for an intsant the whole fury of the cosmic storm seemed to hold its breath. Turning, she stared at grim Bram with eyes in which lurked no malice, no hate . . . only puzzlement . . .

And then her knees sagged. She bent and fell from the roof, her body a golden blur in the streaming rain. She struck far below, on the cobbles, and the Jewel fell with her, a flashing spark of weird light.

For a long moment the light held, and they stared down at the red, broken thing on the cobbles far below . . . the wet horror that had once been so young, so fair . . . and then a wave of darkness fell.

Chandar felt a hot rage growing within him. Not rage against Bram, who had done what he had to do, but rage at the very nature of things, that demanded such a thing be done. He let the rage feed the growing strength within him to a hot core of inner fire.

He lifted the Axe before his eyes, and spoke the Words of Power. A tide of measureless force welled from him into the swirling chaos above.

Now the rhythm of battle changed. The Black One was shrinking back now, its talismanic aid gone. Falling back before the blinding bolts of lightning that thundered against the dark shield, hammering through.

Chandar poured his strength against the Dark Flame. The fiery hammer-blows crushed down upon the failing darkness. Again and again the blazing bolts struck home.

How long did it last? Afterward, no one could remember. To Chandar, it seemed as if furious hours poured swiftly past. But at length, Light won. The Darkness weakened, drained of strength. Fiercely probing beams of incandescent force poured upon it—and it shrank. Gradually dwindling, the Dark Flame drew in upon itself, coiling, retreating before the tides of beating flame that hammered against it, as a dark rock is beaten about with a sea of white fire.

Numbly, Chandar held the Axe. His mind was a dead thing. His heart was a cold lump within his breast. His body was dead flesh. Blind, deafened, he stood there like a pillar of stone, pouring forth endless power from deep wells within him, hidden wellsprings of courage and stamina.

He never knew how long it lasted, but after a measureless time he felt Bram's strong arm about his shoulders, and a flask of wine against his numb lips. He gagged, choking at the cold sparkling wine, but as it poured down his throat he felt a warm relaxing fire spread tingling through his cold, beaten flesh, and he felt the weariness bone-deep within him fade beneath a new wave of strength.

He turned from the lips of the wine-flask, gasping for breath, and met Llys' eyes. Her face was wet, flushed, but her eyes were shining softly at him.

"It is over now," she said.

Lifting his eyes, he could see that the skies were clear and deep, the Darkness dispelled, and the first faint rose-golden light of dawn broke against the upper spires of Shiangkor.

13 DAWN OVER SHIANGKOR

THE CITY lay as silent as a dead place beneath the soft light of dawn. Wet streets were littered with rubble . . . and with bodies. The proud fleet was a ruin of shattered hulks, over whose broken hulls the sluggish waves broke slowly. The clouds had cleared away . . . the storm had ebbed and died in a great, peaceful silence.

Bram and Meliander helped Chandar to his feet. He felt tired—every muscle ached with a dull fatigue—but it was not the drained, dead-ash sensation that seemed to follow as the aftermath of using the Axe, but a normal weariness, the sort of wholesome tiredness that follows in the wake of hard work.

His head felt clear. His heart beat strongly.

"What happened?" he asked.

Meliander bowed his head.

"Naught, but that the Flame triumphed and the Darkness . . . went back to wherever it came from. The Flame tells us that it will never arise to trouble this world of Iridar again."

"Never?" Chandar's voice rang with the strength of a new manhood. For iron had entered him during his great fight; he was a man now, a youth no more.

"Never," Meliander answered slowly, "until the Last Days have come, and this world goes forth into the great dark that lies beyond all light. The Flame has promised this to us. The Shadow has lifted here—forever."

A fresh breeze blew from the sea, with the clean tang of salt air. Dawn grew slowly, unfolding like a golden rose in the eastern skies.

Bram's eyes were humble.

"I had to do it, lad. You know that. It had to be done."

"I know . . ."

"When the shadows fell, I knew it was the K'thomi wench. I took up a fallen sword and went out to hunt her. She had to be slain, and that quickly."

"Yes."

"Say you forgive me, lad?"

Chandar laid his hand on Bram's shoulder.

"Say no more about it. It had to be done . . . and, had it been my task . . . I am not sure I could have done it. No, I hold it not against you, my oldest friend. I owe my life to you, many times over. One death shall not wipe out that debt."

Llys regarded him with gentle eyes.

"Was she . . . much . . . to you?"

Chandar drew a deep breath, and let it go out of him slowly. For a moment he said nothing, then he shook his head.

"She was nothing to me. She could have been . . . much. Perhaps. I cannot say. Because that which might have been between us did not have time enough to be born. Speak no more of it; it is done and over."

"Thank the Great Gods for that!" Bram murmured softly in his beard.

Below them, on the streets, the people were coming out from their hiding places, by twos and threes. There was a cowed, beaten look about them. They gathered together in small groups, standing silently looking at one another's faces, or staring at the clear, brightening sky. They slowly began drifting towards the castle.

Meliander coughed, breaking Chandar's reverie.

"Let us go down into the Hall, and speak to the people. Many things have changed this night of all our nights. And the Flame would speak, for he is there below."

Chandar nodded, and slipped an arm about Llys's slender waist. They left the balcony and went down a flight of stone steps into the vast Hall, where the dead body of Niamnon still lay face-downward in a puddle of blood . . . his crushed crown beside him.

Some of the counselors and lords had already entered the Hall, and stood far off, gazing silently at the fallen King. They did not speak, until Meliander, Chandar, Llys and Bram came into the Hall.

One elderly noble recognized the Wizard.

"It is the Lord Meliander, that was driven forth from his Kingdom years ago!" he cried.

Meliander bowed slightly.

"Lord Norcandir, I remember you well."

"So you have returned! It is good. The ancient blood shall rule our land again, even though the King is fallen."

"That lies in other hands than mine," Meliander said. And he led his companions across the Hall to the foot of the dais where the empty throne stood, waiting.

Now the Hall was slowly filling with the townsfolk. Pale nobles and hushed guardsmen were there, as well as sturdy peasants and tradesmen, merchants and artisans, and the men of the guilds and the fleet. They all seemed subdued, shaken by the cosmic events of the night. The imperial pride was gone from them, beaten out of their minds and spirits by the great winds and fierce lightning blows that had shaken the city itself.

In the city of Shiangkor an age had ended, and a new age was about to begin.

At the foot of the dais they paused. Meliander slowly climbed the steps and stood, looking out over the now crowded hall. He raised his hands for silence.

"The days of Niamnon are ended, and the Throne lies empty. Many things have changed in this pastnight, and we must now decide the direction of the future. Speak!"

Norcandir, Elder of the Council and wise Illondus the Lore Master stepped forward.

"Lord Meliander! You are the last of the blood of your House, the Son of Pohlindandar, the Son of Terinth. When your mighty Sire died, the Throne of Shiangkor was your rightful inheritance. Your younger brother seized it by force, deposing you and forcing you to flee for your life. But now the tyrant is dead, and you have returned from your exile . . . why, then, shall you not rule over us? What say the people to this?"

Lord Norcandir turned to the crowd, but ere they could speak, Meliander lifted one hand.

"I am old, and shall get no children to carry on my House. Therefore I shall not take the Throne."

The Lore Master spoke up: "Do you then suggest that the Noble Houses of the realm select one of their number to assume the Kingship? But, Lord Prince, that will bring dissension and blood-feud, plotting and counter-plotting . . . the realm will be torn with factions, divided against itself, if one House is given precedence over all the rest, who are equal to it in station."

Meliander nodded, gravely.

"Well said, wise Illondus. But I offer no such solution. Mine is a different answer."

He turned to Chandar, who stood silently at the foot of the dais, with Llys and Bram by his side.

"This man you all know, Prince Chandar of Orm, the Son of Guthrum, the Son of Gondomyr. He is young, brave, strong—keen of mind and stout of heart. It was his hand that felled the tyrant, Niamnon. Let the Crown pass to his brow, and that Lady, Llys of Iophar, become his Queen. Strong sons shall they raise, to inherit this land and rule it with justice and wisdom. I have spoken."

The crowd burst into speech, neighbor turning to dispute with neighbor, and at length they stilled. The elder nobles stepped forward to kneel before Chandar of Orm. In turn, he placed his hand briefly upon each head.

Chandar then ascended to the level of the Throne of Shiangkor, standing beside Meliander. The old Wizard bent to kneel in homage before his King, but Chandar stayed him with a stern gesture.

"Kneel not to me, friend! But stay, and rule this city in my place, as my equal."

"Lord King!" the Elder cried from below. "Do you then, too, renounce kingship? What shall become of Shiangkor?"

Chandar spoke.

"Have you not had enough of Empire in all these bloody years of conquest?" he demanded fiercely. "Do you not tire beneath the weight of so many crowns? Your King, Niamnon, led you to the rape of white Delphontis beside the entrance of Kalunda Val, the Inner Sea, and of Illionis to the north . . . and ravished my own homeland of Orm. House after House was unkinged with the sword and the fiery stake. Let us have an end to these Kings-of-Kings! I will wear no crown but that of my father, Guthrum of Orm. But if you will king me, then hear my first decree: from this hour forward, the Empire of Shiangkor is no more. Delphontis, Orm, and all the Kingdoms which have been brought under the sceptre of Shiangkor, I command to renounce that sceptre and declare them free and independent states once more . . . free to choose their own Kings and to follow them. Shiangkor I take as a realm subject to Orm, and I deliver it as a fief into the keeping of Lord Meliander, who shall rule here in my place, despite his modest wish to withdraw."

The crowd thundered.

Above the noise, Chandar roared: "The legions of Shiangkor I disband, and the fleets I disperse . . . what little of them is left, after the great storm. And this I have spoken."

And then—in a sudden silence—another voice spoke, silvery, musical.

"I too shall speak."

Above the crowd, a dancing white Flame appeared,

dazzling phantom of purest light. It descended to hover
above the empty Throne.

*"It is my will that the commands of Chandar, Prince of
Orm and Shiangkor, be obeyed. The Empire is no more,
and the kingdoms conquered by Niamnon may either re-
vert to the remnants of their former Royal Houses, or
choose a new monarch from among their nobles."*

The singing voice was heard in a deathly hush. The
Shiangkori craned to see the weirdly beautiful, immortal
Being whose enormous powers had been so impressively
demonstrated on the night just ended. Its wishes were
hearkened to in a respectful silence.

*"The Axe of Orm shall remain an Arch-Talisman of
power, and its power—which is my power—I place at the
disposal of Chandar the King. With it in his hands, and
in the hands of his sons, peace shall be kept in these
northern lands. But know that the House of the Ormslings
is under my especial protection . . . and that from his Blood
shall arise a race of mighty Kings, the* Jalangir Thon, *who
shall one day—be it late or be it soon—unite these realms
into a mighty Empire. That is my wish, and my prophecy
to the people of Iridar. Heed me well."*

"Aye, Lord!" the people answered, in a many-throated
murmur. They bowed before the Flame, heads bobbing
as the sheaves of grain bow before a slow wave of wind.

The Flame ascended into the heights above the Hall.

*"Meliander, once of Shiangkor and then of Iophar, be
now the Lord of Shiangkor again, even as Chandar the
King has decreed!"*

"Aye, Great One," Meliander bowed.

*"And when your long days have reached their end at
last, see that the elder son of Chandar the King inherits
your Throne, so that the blood of the House of Orm shall
gain empery over this land of Shiangkor that has so griev-
ously felt my wrath, and, so doing, this land too shall come
beneath my protection."*

Meliander bowed.

*"Chandar, King of Orm, and Ilys, that was Queen of
Iophar and shall henceforth be Queen of Ormsgard—farewell to you. Reign with mercy, justice and industry, and my
good wishes shall go ever out to you and to yours!"*

Chandar bowed. Llys stretched out her arms imploringly to the Flame.

"Lord! What shall become of my lost Kingdom? Who shall rule the Land of Magic in my stead?"

"Fear not, Lady. The Lord Iombis of that realm shall ascend the Crystal Throne, and his children shall rule wisely and well."

"Shall we then, never look on you again, Lord?" Chandar asked. The Flame danced.

"Summon me to see your first-born, by that means your Lady, who was and is my Servant, well knows. But now,— farewell! I am weary from my wars, and will come unto my cavern once again, and there shall sleep a time—I, who have never slept—while I rebuild my full strength. Fare- well, Meliander of Shiangkor—Bram, red bear of Orm, farewell! And farewell, King and Queen of Orm—awaken me to see your first-born son!"

The Flame ascended to the vaulted roof and passed through a great window into the open air and was gone. With his going, a great sigh breathed from the throng that had stood so long, hushed in the awe of his presence.

Chandar watched the Flame until it vanished from sight, and then he turned to Llys. Tears stood like bright jewels in her eyes . . . eyes as blue as the cornflower, veiled be- neath soft hair the color of sunlight.

He took her in his arms.

"All will come true, even as the Flame has spoken," he whispered. "My love—my Queen, whom I have loved from that first hour I awakened in the pearl chambers of Iophar to gaze into the eyes of her I thought a nurse—and whom I have loved from that moment to this, and shall love for all my life hereafter—we shall call the Flame when our first-born draws breath in the Queen's Chamber of Orms- gard, above the ice blue waters of the fjord."

A rosy hue mantled her white throat, and dim lashes dropped over her eyes.

"And have you loved me so?" she said, softly. "Then learn that from that hour that you awoke, the unknown outland stranger from the sea, your face has been before my eyes—your name within my heart—and I have loved you from that moment to this, and shall love no other man so long as I, too, live."

She raised her lids and her blue eyes shone softly into his. And her rose lips parted to speak again . . . but he silenced them gently, with their first kiss.

Bram roared, and flung his arms about the smiling Lord Meliander's neck.

"What a world, my Master!" he chuckled. "Adventure over half a world, and at the end of all lies ever a crown, a maiden, and a kingdom! Ah, what a world!"

Meliander smiled.

"It is ever thus, friend Bram, when hearts are young and blood flows swift to the trumpet call of adventure. Begrudge them not their youth, for ere the year be out, your arms, too, will be full with a wife."

Bram's jaw gaped.

"Say you in truth?"

Meliander nodded, chuckling. The red-bearded giant rubbed his cheek, musing.

"A Wizard's word . . . I do not call you liar, Lord, but . . . I have become cursed weary of magic in these days since Kralian plucked us from the deep!"

Above them, parting from their embrace, the King and Queen of Orm smiled laughing down at Bram's embarrassed face, as crimson as his beard.

The people thundered in ovation, making the ancient rafters of the Hall ring. Swords hissed from scabbards and were raised along and massed voices boomed the ancient and heart-stirring cry:

"Hail King! Reign King! May the King reign forever!"

And through the great windows, the full light of morning poured into the bloody Hall. Clear and fresh and bright with infinite promise, the glory of dawn blazed over Shiangkor beside the mighty sea.

EPILOGUE

But of course, no story ever really ends with a neat, final scene . . . and all its characters entering at last a life of peace and happiness. Nor did this story of the first of the race of the JALANGIR THON—*the Great Kings.*

For a month, Meliander feasted Chandar and Llys in Shiangkor. And then, with Bram beside them, and leading a loyal host of troops, they returned to Orm on its rock-bound headland beyond the Gates of the Inner Sea —broke the legions occupying the land—rebuilt the sacked castle—and brought the scattered people together once again. With his own hands, Chandar lifted again into its ancient place the great fire-blackened kingpost of the Hall, whereon his father had died many years before. And, in time, in that same Hall, he made Llys of Iophar his wife and his Queen, by the ancient liturgies of his nation.

Nor did the legions of Shiangkor in yet other parts of the extinct Empire, tamely lay down their swords when heralds brought the commands of Chandar and Meliander. And so the next year he must go forth to war again, this time leading a combined host of troops from Orm, Nemour, Delphontis and the other near realms of the North, against the rebels—whom he overwhelmed in time, but not without much labor and many battles, and not without awakening the supernatural energies of the Axe of Power once again.

Nor were the Kingdoms of the North content to merely honor the victorious King of Orm with empty triumphs and festivals, upon his return. In the first Great Council-of-Kings, the newly created Kings of northernmost Orcys by the river Dashpar, of sea-girt Illionis and of mighty Shiangkor, of white Delphontis and proud Nemour gratefully conferred upon the sixth King of their company a title also newly created . . . and Chandar of Orm (whom

98

the joyous peoples of the Northern coasts were already beginning to hail as CHANDAR JALANGIR—*"Chandar the Great") became the first High-King of the Septentrion, and by that name we must call the six Kingdoms of the North for from that date so were they known.*

In time, as is the way of women, the Queen Llys became a mother and her son, Prince Aomar, was made Heir to Shiangkor upon the express wish of the Flame. And the following year, while the High-King was far to sea, subduing the remnants of the Imperial fleets, who had taken refuge in those same Hundred Isles where once the young Chandar long ago had been Prince of Corsairs and were now battling for supremacy with the last of those same corsairs, Chandar's old comrades,—she became a mother for the second time, and bore the Prince Thar, who became Heir to Ormsgard. So that when the High-King at length returned to his land, with the Lord Admiral Bram (newly wed, and soon to be a father himself) by his side and a host of his old pirate-comrades who would form the nucleus of the Orm Fleet . . . he found himself a father twice-over.

Meliander the King visited his Lord later that year to see his friends once again, and to dandle upon his knee the Heir to Shiangkor. And there was high feasting under the ancient rafters of Ormsgard Hall, when old friends and new friends came together once again. Prince Thar squalled lustily, but his elder brother accepted the uproar with all the aplomb and detachment of one born to Kingship.

It was this same Thar, Son of Chandar (you may remember), who was many years later to go forth on the famous Quest of the Sword of Psamathis, where he discovered the age-old terror of . . .

. . . But that's another story!

THE END

Peril of the Starmen

1

"I CALLED you three in," the Oligarch said, "because I have some very important news."

Herb—he would later be assigned that name—was one of the three. He hated the Oligarch, and he had no doubt that the Oligarch knew it.

"There are," the Oligarch said, "people on the planet. Unfortunately."

Dull rage and frustration and despair and helplessness bubbled up in Herb. His face remained calm.

"We'll have to keep them from interfering with us," the Oligarch said.

Herb wanted to cry: Find another! Not this one! Not the only one we've ever found with people on it!

But he said nothing. His anguished thoughts whirled like a dust storm, handling and rejecting ideas like bits of paper. The remote and inaccessible Scientists were beyond accounting. Perhaps only this planet would serve. Perhaps there was insufficient time to locate another of suitable mass. Perhaps . . . But one could not know. One could only submit to authority. The storm died away, and Herb acknowledged bitter reality with helplessness. There even seemed a nightmare inevitability about the selection.

"It would be dangerous to try to work secretly," the Oligarch said. "If they were to discover us in the midst of planting the explosive, it would be fatal. We'll go down and ask their permission."

No one protested.

"To that end," the Oligarch said, "I have selected you three competent, trustworthy men. You will learn their language and when we land, lull their natural suspicions.

101

It will be your responsibility to see that we blow up the planet on schedule."

The crush of the responsibility was terrifying. "I don't need to tell you," the Oligarch said, "that you can't fail."

And it was true. Herb *believed*.

Unless the planet Earth were exploded, the ever-unstable Universe, itself, would collapse. Already the binding force was dangerously diminished. If new energy were not released within a month, disintegration would begin. The Universe would alter and flow and contract and after the collapse, slowly build itself into a new form—that form itself containing the inherent stresses of change and mutability. Only the arrival of starmen to space flight at the critical time—only their continued vigilance—prevented disaster beyond accounting for.

Herb *believed*.

2

WELL INSIDE the solar system the huge space ship plunged on, released from the warp drive and slowly braking to establish an orbit around the third planet.

Herb came up from the deep stupor of the drugs. He had been under their influence for the last twenty hours while the sleep tapes hammered information into his unconscious brain.

"All right," said Wezen, their private custodian, "time for exercise. Two hours of work-outs, and then you eat."

Herb sat up and felt his head. It ached dully. "Give me a minute. Time to think, Wezen. I'm—"

The other two starmen were also recovering.

"None of that! No time to think! Get up! Get up!"

Herb got reluctantly to his feet. Cold air washed over his nude body, and he trembled. He wanted to return to sleep, not the drugged sleep of the sleep tapes, but the genuine, untroubled sleep. Something frightening and alien was taking place in his mind.

He looked around for a dream form. It was a subconscious response. He realized with relief that it was not necessary to fill one in. Technically, he had not been asleep.

The Oligarch came to witness the first awakening. "How goes it, Wezen?"

"Fine."

"I don't know," Herb said. "My mind, it's . . . I can't think . . ."

One of the others said, "There's all kinds of information, but I can't get at it. I . . . can't . . . get . . . at . . . it." He looked around desperately. "Every time I try, something new comes up. It's like a volcano. I can't control it. I think, the name of a river is Mississi—and then I know that leaves are green, and . . ."

"The sun is 93 million miles away. . . ."

"The day is divided into twenty-four equal periods of sixty minutes . . ."

"The largest ocean is the Pacific . . ."

"The Federal Government, of the United States of America is composed of three independent branches . . ."

They were all talking at once.

"It's awful. Not to be able to control . . ."

"Good, good," said the Oligarch. He was satisfied with the progress. By the time they landed, they would be little more than mechanisms designed to answer questions; they would not be able to think at all: they would *respond*. Stimuli-response.

"Freedom," said the Oligarch.

"Is," Herb found himself saying, "is the basis of any government that governs justly."

Wezen made a little intake of air that was loud in the shocked silence.

"I said that," Herb said unbelievingly.

"Excellent," said the Oligarch. "The proper reaction."

Wezen relaxed, but he was visibly shaken. He had *heard* the heresy. What might happen to him later, when this job was done?

"The indoctrination is beginning nicely." The Oligarch nodded. They would be able to soothe suspicion and dispel fear when they arrived on Earth. They would speak of love and assistance when the time came. "But you will have much to learn."

"You have a lot of information about them," Herb said. "Their history . . . their . . . You got it just in the last few days from their radio and television shows? I don't see how . . ."

"We extrapolate; there are machines," the Oligarch said. He regarded Herb narrowly. "I believe we better step up the pace." He was not going to give Herb time to rest, to think, to understand, to correlate the mind staggering mass of information he was receiving. "Let's hurry to the recreation room for calisthenics."

In the corridor, Herb glanced around for microphones and saw he was in an unwired stretch. He turned to the starman beside him. Their eyes met. Identical information had been fed simultaneously to both of them. "You heard what I said?"

"Yes."

"What kind of a place is this, this Earth?"

The other strained to think. "It's . . . It's . . . I don't believe it."

"All men are created equal," Herb said.

"And they hold these truths to be self evident . . ."

"Nor make any laws abridging . . ."

"Shhhhh!" the third starman whispered. "Microphones up here."

They fell silent.

The Oligarch went to his stateroom and ordered a meal. He had been indoctrinated by the sleep tapes about Earth well over a Brionimanian year previously. The tapes had been brought back by an extensive scouting expedition composed solely of Oligarchs.

He found them a naive race. Weakness, of course, was their shortcoming. As was often the case. He imagined his hand touching the lever that would trigger the explosive. He saw, in imagination, the planet fly asunder.

He had destroyed before. Five races had died beneath his hands. And now—

Perhaps, he thought, I am growing old. Why is it I do

not want to destroy this race myself? Am I becoming weak?

He was angry with himself. Weakness! he thought. I'm acting like a subject, he thought. *I'm an Oligarch.*

Oligarch, he thought.

Five races, and now the sixth . . .

Where will it end? he thought.

It will never end.

Slowly the smile came. We are supreme, he thought, the lords and masters, and it will never end.

His scalp prickled with destiny.

Five races. He saw his hand reach out for the sixth. He shuddered. Weeks ago he had reached his decision. Bleakly he thought: I can't do it.

Perspiration crept down his spine. If a planet were not blown up, the whole fabric of his society would collapse. Brionimar must never learn.

But Brionimar *would* learn. Earth was on the verge of space flight. Within a generation they would be listening for radio and television extension-waves in hyperspace that would indicate the existence of another civilization. In two generations they would be in the skies of Brionimar. And then the subjects would see salvation: here (they would reason) is another race capable of preserving the Universe. And there would be no appeasing their blind and mindless wrath until the last Oligarch was dismembered and bloodless.

His hand reached out and curled around an imaginary lever. It must be done, he thought. But not by me. Not by me. Not this hand. He looked down at his hands: white and immaculate and always clean. He washed them frequently.

Someone else must pull the lever.

I must leave a man behind at the bomb site to do it, he thought.

Psychology was a science on Brionimar; and he was a scientist. There was only one man he could be sure of out of all the crew. There were several fanatics, but he distrusted them. There was one idealist who would, of a psychological certainty, pull that lever and blow himself up along with Earth in the belief that his action was necessary to preserve the Universe.

Herb.

3

WHEN THE starmen came, they made headlines in the newspapers all over the world.

They sat down on the east-west runway of the Washington National Airport.

MEN FROM STARS LAND!

And shortly:

FIRST CONTACT REVEALS STARMEN HUMANOID!
GENERAL SAYS ARMY READY IF STARMEN MENACE!
EARTH WARNS VISITORS!

And on the heels of these:

UNEASINESS SPREADS!
STARMEN SAY PEACE THEIR MISSION!
NO INVASION, SAYS WILKERSON!
PEACE, SAY STARMEN!

And a few hours later:

CONGRESS TO MEET!
CONGRESS FORMS COMMITTEE: WILL REPORT FINDINGS TO AMERICAN PEOPLE!
STARMEN SAY PEACE BETWEEN WORLDS!

Fear and faith combined; courage and cowardice; hatred and optimism. The great ground swell of popular approval was to come much later. At first there was naked uncertainty. Could the starmen be trusted?

And suppose they could be trusted?

Suppose that.

What then?

What?

Many were afraid.

Bud Council, freshman senator from the state of Missouri, was one of them. In the course of events he was to be assigned to the Committee to investigate the Starmen. A weak man, a fearful man, and as such, a dangerous man . . .

4

FROM HIS initial statement it was obvious that Bud sided with the group determined to oppose all contact with the starmen. His reaction was more frantic than most. He awoke at night from a soggy dream of terror. *Let us alone,* he sobbed, trembling. *Let us alone.* The future, once so secure, was now a veiled menace. *Go away,* he whispered into the night, *let us alone. We don't want you. Go away.*

He appeared sleepless for the first hearing. The three starmen filed in. He hated them.

They testified.

Herb, in the witness stand, peered out at the swarm of white faces; his head turned automatically from interrogator to interrogator.

"Our government is a modified democracy, much as your own, containing strong safeguards for individual liberty and civil rights," Herb said. One would need to look deeply into his eyes to detect the dullness and the depersonalization that was the true index to the words.

His thoughts were fuzzy, floating upon the periphery of his immediate existence. A detached part of himself seemed to observe and record the proceedings without understanding them; there was a fever of information inside of him.

"We believe in the mutual exchange of knowledge. As proof of our good will, we will be glad to send in a team of scientists . . ." And later: "Our aim is mutually profitable trade."

He rested. One of the starmen took the stand. The drone and whine of voices lulled Herb. He wanted to relax, to sleep, to recover, to become master of himself once again.

After a recess, he found himself once more on the stand. Senator Rawlins, a thin, nervous mid-Westerner, began a line of inquiry. Herb tested his fingers, feeling the comforting reality of the hard chair arm. He explored the surface with childish wonder while his voice responded and waited and responded. Dimly, persistently, doggedly, stubbornly the ego, the self—that small spark of assertiveness and awareness—struggled to arrange and order, to reason and make sense of—to unify and master—the knowledge it possessed. The consistency with which his spoken lies appealed to human prejudice should have made him realize the extent to which the Oligarchy was experienced in dealing with alien civilizations and the extent to which they had prepared specifically to confront this one. But he was aware only of the sound of his voice. The words fell away into some lost abyss of confusion.

"But the theory behind this, now?" Senator Rawlins said.

"I'm sorry, sir. We are technicians aboard this expedition. We have very little to do with the theoretical aspects. That's up to the Scientists."

"Well, you are, sir, familiar with the idea that—we'll say—that light has limited velocity?"

"Yes, sir, that is correct. It wouldn't make sense for it to have infinite velocity, to be instantaneously everywhere." A tiny sense of urgency formed in his mind.

"Are you familiar with the fact that the speed of light is a limiting factor? Nothing in the natural Universe goes faster than light."

"I couldn't say, sir, I really don't know. At an extremely high speed our space ship makes a, a *transition,* but . . . I guess, sir, yes, sir." The answers weren't coming now. The Oligarch had not dared permit him scientific knowledge. There was a little vacuum where there should be information.

"You'll pardon me, but aren't you unusually ignorant, for a technician, about physical theory: about the action of gases that we were talking about a moment ago—in fact, even about astronomy?"

Herb did not say that such pursuits were the exclusive prerogatives of the Oligarchs. He did not say: I am inferior in mental capacity to an Oligarch; I can never become a Scientist. That was not to be mentioned. "I am a technician, sir."

Senator Rawlins shook his head and made a few notes.

There was fear somewhere inside of him. What more could he say? Suppose . . . suppose . . . Had he answered wrong? It was as if his knowledge were a river rushing his ego toward the great waterfall of defeat, and he was powerless to control anything. He must not fail. Must not, must not, must not fail.

The imminence of collapse made the very sky terrifying, to know that this apparent order could crumble, and planets fly from suns, and suns themselves spin blindly nowhere. Every word before the Committee was vital. The whole wheeling order of existence turned upon it.

He felt the wood beneath his finger tips, smooth and cool and solid.

The second day of the open hearing, Norma flew down from Vermont to reason with Bud.

Bud was gracious. Years in politics had taught him to mask his real feelings; taught him so well that he was no longer at all sure what his real feelings were.

The outbursts of anger and suppressed sadism he unleashed on those closest to him always the morning after confused him and left him feeling that the person of the previous day had been someone distinct and separate from his genuine self.

"It's good to see you," he said. A warm, brotherly and artificial love flattered his sense of rectitude. He considered her the baby of the family. He remembered her as a gawky, frightened girl giving a last long glance at the security of the living room before venturing into the night of her first date. "I've been meaning to get up your way." His hands signaled the extent of his confinement to Washington. "There's so much to do, you can't imagine. I have to take work home with me. I'm sometimes up half the night with it . . . I've been hearing about you. Very fine, Norma, very fine."

Norma was tense and uncomfortable and, Bud thought, a little overawed to be sitting across the desk from her own brother in the rebuilt Senate Office Building.

She blinked nervously: "Frank will be in this afternoon."

"Yes. Yes?" A trace of petulance haunted Bud's voice. "Terribly busy just now, but . . ." Hollow enthusiasm conquered. "That's just fine. I can always find time to see Frank."

"He thinks it's important that he see you," Norma said.

"Has something happened?" Bud always sought ways to escape from the anticipated responsibility of sharing a family crisis.

"We want to talk to you."

"I don't quite understand, Norma. What are you talking about?"

"These hearings, Bud."

Instantly the Senator felt the crush of the whole family arrayed against him, and he wanted to snarl at her in shame and anger and shout, "Leave me alone! Leave me alone! Leave me alone, for Chrissake!"

"They've got space flight. We can't even begin to guess what else they've got. What does Senator Stilson do? And you're there on his side, right with him!"

Bud puffed his cheeks and his skin grew hot and prickly. *It's none of your damned business,* he thought viciously.

"They have space flight," she repeated doggedly. "Think what that would mean to us."

"I haven't time to discuss it right now, Sis. We'll have to talk this out later." He stood up, anger pounding in his temples.

She stood with him. "Tonight. You and I and Frank."

"I don't quite see how . . ." His voice was weary, and he let the sentence hang short of blunt refusal.

"Tonight, Bud. We've got to see you tonight. He's flying in."

"Well . . ." he sighed resignedly. "My place, then. I'll see you at, nine o'clock there."

"That will be fine."

"Nine, then. I've got to rush. My place at nine."

"Goodby, Bud."

Less than an hour later flash bulbs popped from all corners of the room as the starmen entered for their second session of questioning.

Chairman Stilson, in a peevishly thin voice, limited the photographers to ten minutes and ruled against pictures during the questioning. After nearly half an hour, the hearing got under way.

Herb was first on the stand. He continued in the same fashion as yesterday. His answers were polite and informative. Senator Stilson's attempt to get him to contradict himself proved unfruitful. Herb surrendered the chair to one of the others and returned to his seat at the long table reserved for the starmen.

The hearing droned on. He no longer listened. He wanted to sleep.

"Yes," said the starman who was testifying, "that is correct. One of our main reasons for making this expedition is to offer you technological information: space flight, medicine . . ."

". . . eventually trade . . ."

"Initiate a cultural exchange at the first practical moment . . ."

Herb heard someone say: "But we have limited facilities on this expedition. A larger one, with your permission, will be dispatched for Earth within a year." He was not even sure whether it was he who was speaking. "In the meantime, we would like permission to conduct certain scientific tests on the surface . . . A mineral analysis, sir, primarily. But we are interested in geological evidence . . ."

". . . whether or not," someone said, "the physical similarity of our two races is due to parallel evolution or to a forgotten, prehistoric cycle of colonization by a common ancestor . . ."

". . . These tests can be completed within a few days . . ."

"In return, sir, we offer . . ."

". . . We must leave within a week. We must have an answer before then."

They described their own planet and their own civilization. They made an excellent impression.

When it was Bud's turn to question, he asked Herb: "How do we know—here, you've learned the language, so much about us and all—how do we know that this isn't a fabrication, a tissue of prevarications you're telling the American people here today? We have to take everything on faith. Now, you know so much about us, you have studied us . . ."

"We have only a week . . ." Herb replied.

They were waiting for Bud at nine o'clock. He was late.

"I'm sorry," Bud said. "Came as quickly as I could. I was at a secret session . . . But for a brother and sister, well, I just had to leave . . ."

"We appreciate it, Bud," Norma said.

"Drink, anybody?"

"No, thanks," Frank said.

Norma shook her head.

"Mind if I have one? I'm rather upset today—the hearings and all, the meeting tonight . . ."

He went to his bar.

Frank was on the sofa. His gaunt, heavy boned body waited motionless. His blunt fingered, surgeon's hands lay unmoving. His skin was tanned from the Oklahoma sun. Norma sat stiffly erect in the overstuffed chair.

"I guess you know what we want to see you about," Frank said.

Bud poured carefully without looking around. "Norma said something about the starmen. Terrifying thing, terrifying thing. You think they'll really leave when we tell them to?"

"I don't see there's much we can do about it if they make up their minds to stay," Frank said.

"Look, Bud," Norma said, "think how far ahead of us they are. They must be friendly, they must be sincere in their offer to help us."

Bud shook his head. "My deep and sincere conviction on this is that it's a matter of our pride and our independ-

ence and our freedom. They're all at stake. I mean—"
He waved helplessly. "You know how I feel. I mean, my
views are in all the papers, in the *Record*. With me it's a
matter of principle. I dont' see how we can accept that sort
of offer. It's degrading."

"If we tell them to leave, to go away, to leave us alone,
we've lost the greatest opportunity in history." Norma in-
sisted.

"Norma," Bud said. "You know how I feel about you.
You know I'd do anything in the world for either of you.
Anything within my power. All you need do is ask. Money,
anything. But this . . . this . . . We're proud. Mankind is
proud." His heart swelled with the beauty of renunciation
and righteousness. "We're too proud, too independent, too
free. I would not be willing to sacrifice those great, eternal
truths, those historic principles that are the foundation of
our way of life, that have made America great: dignity,
pride, self reliance . . ."

"I think they have about the same metabolism as humans," Frank said. "Speaking as a medical man, I believe
if they'd give us their medical knowledge, we could con-
quer disease on Earth. And with their technology—"

"We are a proud race," Bud said. "We must cling to
that. That is more precious than gold."

When Frank spoke, there was a mixture of contempt
and terror in his voice. "Bud, you're a monument to the
basic anarchy of the American people."

"Frank!" Norma cried.

"He is. If the people paid any attention to what they
were doing, do you think they'd elect a man like that?"

Bud's mind darted frantically. What was happening here?
What was behind this? Why was Frank, his own brother,
out to get him? What sinister motive—?

"You underestimate them, though," Frank said. There's
a little trickle of maturity in this country. For every aberra-
tion like you it gains a drop of experience and knowledge.
The war is over. We've had our emotional jag. We're about
to go into one of our rational periods. We're about to wake
up to our responsibilities. Your day is passing. I don't know
if there's enough of you left to keep out the starmen. The

people are coming around. But—I—do—know—this. I know . . ."

"Stop!" Norma cried. "You don't understand Bud! You're trying to make him into something dishonest and cynical!"

"I've watched him come up. I've watched him for years. I've seen all the rotten deals he's pulled. I've seen him smear innocent people—ruin their careers—and all not for patriotism but for himself. To advance his career. Keep his name before the public. He doesn't care for anything but Bud. Bud, and any means to the end that he moves up, gets power—power for power's sake—power to create and destroy—power to change and control. I've watched him: I know him. I'm talking the only language he understands."

Bud was trembling. The sense of indignation, horror, and innocence was blunted by the shallow dryness of his breathing.

"Frank! Stop this! You're out of your mind!"

"I'm going to see you defeated in the next election, Bud. I'm going to dig up dirt, I'm going to find out who your mistresses are. I'm your brother. I'm going to hound you, disgrace you, drive you from office. You know me. You know I mean what I say. You know me. You know I mean what I say. *You know I will do it."*

"What do you want? My, my God, Frank, what are you after?"

Frank's hands were shaking. His mouth worked nervously. "For once in my life, for once in my life I've got something all-the-way decent to fight for, and I mean to fight just as dirty as I have to get it. Bud, you're coming over to my side on this starmen hearing. You're going to vote for co-operation with them. Do you hear me? Do you hear what I say?"

Bud, his eyes bulging with shock and disbelief, shook his head dumbly. His own brother—this terror raging before him—impossible, his own brother . . . His heart pounded. His will was gone. "What do you want?" he repeated dryly.

"I told you."

"I—I—I'll have to think. I—I—"

"No you won't," Frank said. He stood before him now. "No, you won't."

Norma jumped between them. "Leave him alone!"

Bud snaked from behind her and fled to the bar. His unprotected back a crawling mass of chill, he poured himself a drink. "You're . . . you're upset, Frank. You've been, been overworked." He drank the drink in a feverish gulp. "Now . . ." his voice fluttered nervously. "I'll forget what you've said here tonight. I understand." His breathing was still tight and frightened. "About the starmen. I haven't, I haven't really given the matter too, too much . . . attention. I still have an . . . I was just today thinking of . . ."

Frank started to speak.

"I can see both sides of the argument," Bud said rapidly. In the depth of his stomach he lived with the cold knowledge that Frank would stoop to anything—any lie, any distortion—to—defeat him. Frank could defeat him. It wasn't as if Frank were a stranger. It wasn't as if Bud had been in the Senate for years. No, he was a vulnerable freshman, and unscrupulous politicians back home were already . . . This was terrible. All his dreams of the future trembled on his words. He was physically afraid.

"Frank is upset!" Norma said frantically.

"Yes, yes," Bud murmured.

"Frank, you apologize! You hear me! Apologize!"

Frank and Bud found their eyes locked in a moment of silent communication, and seeing victory in the dull defeat inside of Bud, Frank said hoarsely, "I apologize, Bud. I'm sorry. I shouldn't have said those things. I lost my head. I'm sorry."

They both knew it was no apology. The threat was still very much there.

5

THE SPIDER ships towered above the surrounding aircraft. Their construction was utilitarian; their living quarters were cramped; entrance was achieved from the ground by means of a retractable ladder from the base platform.

The underbelly dome contained the cutting ray. It could strike deep into the Earth, burning through shale and granite with equal efficiency. The portable casing could be sunk almost simultaneously; it would seem to contain the ray as a hose contains water. While like a giant rig, the ship would poise on its triple legs above the operation. As rapidly as the crew could section the casing, the drilling would proceed.

The three ships would form a triangle. Like insects sending down stingers they would, when the time came, lance three deep shafts into the Earth. Then down the casings would plunge the identical charges. Technicians could compute the point where the three shock waves would meet. A fourth ray would enter the Earth to the proper depth; and at that point would be buried the deadly atomic seed. At the proper time, the charges would be detonated. And where their waves met, under incredible heat and pressure, there the chain reaction would begin, to explode, in an instant, the whole of the Earth.

The Oligarch summoned Herb. "You may sit at my table," he said.

Sleep ladened, Herb sank down across from the Oligarch.

"The necessity for rushing them into a hasty decision is unfortunate," the Oligarch said.

Herb sat hating. The words scarcely penetrated into his confused being. The turmoil was worse than ever.

". . . I have been studying the reports. Three members of the Committee, as it stands now, oppose us. And listen . . ."

"Yes."

"They will be sure to try to end the hearings tomorrow."

"Yes," Herb repeated dully.

"It will go to the full Senate. We have requested a decision within a week. That may not be sufficient time for the popular sentiment of the country to crystallize in our favor. A few determined men may be able to defeat us."

Herb felt a little shudder crawl along his mind. Then his thoughts whirled away.

"It will be infinitely more difficult to win the crucial support of Senators Klein, Stilson and Council after the Committee hearings end. We must bring them to our side.

They have become the focal point of the opposition. We must prolong the Committee hearings until we have convinced them. If we can convince them, the full Senate will go along. We'll have ripped the heart out of the opposition."

Herb tried to concentrate on the reasoning. "Yes," he said.

"They will press for an immediate vote. They have known, even if they don't realize it consciously, that the longer they delay, the surer they are of being defeated."

"If we don't . . . can't . . ."

I don't know, the Oligarch thought. *I don't know. Threats? Try to plant the charges secretly?* "We'll have to convince them. And we've got to do it within a week— maybe a little more, a day or two more."

"What do we do? How? I mean, what do we tell them?" Herb's thoughts were like fog. He wished he could go back to sleep.

The Oligarch knew he was wasting his time explaining to Herb. He wished that he could go before the Committee, himself, but he dared not. Automatic reactions were far more consistent and convincing than his calculating deceit would be. *He* could conceivably be caught in a lie. Not Herb.

"I'll . . . I'll try . . ."

The Oligarch analyzed Herb's potential. *Ten days. Ten days. If he becomes unreliable, where shall I find another?*

"We have almost three weeks," Herb said. "We could give them fifteen or sixteen days . . . We could plant the charges in one day . . ."

"You may as well go back to sleep, Herb."

"Yes."

Herb stood up and stumbled away.

The Oligarch returned to his cabin, washed his hands, and went to his desk.

He fumbled at the newspapers. He saw an editorial: "Council Makes Starmen Hearing Political Football." The people were slowly coming to the starmen's support, but how long, how long . . . ? He saw another headline: STAR-MEN POSSIBLE MENACE TO EARTH SOCIETY.

The first thing Herb did upon arising the morning of the third hearing was to fill in his dream form. He had filled in thousands of them during his life, and yet it was always a frightening experience.

A chill of the Unknown confronted him.

Watchful eyes were, in a way, reassuring; planted microphones could be circumvented; spies could be recognized. But the dream form could not be cheated.

What awful secrets did it reveal? Life and death hung in the balance. Somehow they could tell from the fantasy fiction of a dream how you felt about the reality around you: about the Oligarchy, about your job, about your family.

And they could tell when you lied.

And if you said you didn't dream.

Everyone on Brionimar dreamed.

If they didn't like your dreams, they shot you . . .

Even into his numb and information filled mind, terror crept as his pencil moved across the dream form.

He breakfasted in the messhall and then left for the hearing. As usual, there was a group of humans standing outside the guard lines, marveling at the three starships, standing upon spider legs, looking ready to whirl skyward at any sign of hostility. Far above, the interstellar ship waited in the coldness of space for the shuttle ships to complete their mission and return.

There was an unexpected buzz in the Committee Room when Herb and his two companions arrived.

An ugly television camera squatted across from the Chairman's desk.

Bud had changed his vote on televising the hearings.

Herb watched Bud cross to Senator Stilson. Until this morning the two had seemed very friendly.

"Let's get together later," Bud was saying. "I'll explain my position. I'm sure you'll understand."

Senator Stilson refused to acknowledge that Bud was there.

"Look, Eddy, boy, don't act like that. Listen, I was thinking this over last night, and I think it's only right . . ."

"The Socialists have gotten to you, Bud. That's all there is to say."

Bud swallowed in shocked disbelief. "Oh, now . . ." More than anything else in the world Bud wanted to refute this slander. Desperation gripped him: *the socialists have gotten to you!* No! God damn you! Take that back, you son of a bitch! His hands clenched.

He swallowed again, stiffly, with difficulty. Relax. For the love of God, relax. "Oh, now . . ."

Senator Stilson walked away.

Bud sat down weakly. I'll show him, he thought. I'll . . . I'll . . . It was frightening to have Senator Stilson call you a Socialist.

Bud tried not to think about Frank's face . . . Frank's threats had nothing to do with him changing his mind. A man can change his mind. That he *had* changed his mind seemed to Bud a measure of his honesty and fairness. It was nothing less than that.

One of the other starmen whispered to Herb: "That one's changed sides."

Herb nodded. The Senators were beginning to respond to pressure from their constituents. But even as the tension was sinking, even as elation rose, a second emotion swept through him. It was not enough to deceive those in this room. Now he must also lie to innocent watching millions all over the planet. His fists clenched. He hated Bud.

Early in his testimony he noticed a girl in the audience. There was something in her face that made his eyes return to it time after time. Gradually he came to concentrate exclusively on her and try to explain everything to her alone. He smiled uncertainly, and she smiled back encouragement.

And Norma—this situation suddenly became immediate and personal to her. She watched Herb, listening intently, wanting desperately to communicate her encouragement to him and her belief in him.

Bud caught a taxi to attend the executive session of the hearings that had been set for eight o'clock that evening. The starmen would not be present.

Bud was ill at ease. "Hurry up, damn it!" he snapped at his driver.

Telegrams from all over the country had been pouring into his office. They had awakened him to certain possibilities. His changed vote on television had brought him unprecedented publicity, even from normally hostile newspapers. He realized that the longer the hearings continued the more familiar his name would become.

He was convinced by now that the majority of the people (even as himself) were inclined to approve an agreement with the starmen.

Surely they weren't thinking of ending the hearings and taking the matter to the full Senate? They wouldn't dare flush headlines down the drain like that.

Would they?

He grumbled to himself. Of course they wouldn't. Here was a fulcrum, a lever . . .. Look at the publicity . . . After all, another Missourian had made it from a Congressional Committee. Perhaps the starmen hearings had really seized the imagination of the American people . . .

He experienced a moral awakening, a sharp clear call to duty that transcended morality. All things changed. The world was suddenly portentous and thrilling, and secret enemies lurked and unseen disasters hovered.

His mind was humming with the exultation. He thought of himself dying at the end of his . . . sixth . . . eighth . . . tenth . . . term of office. He pictured the universal sorrow. He wanted to cry. They would mourn for a year; for two years. They would build huge monuments to his memory. Monuments bigger than any monuments ever built.

The taxi stopped.

Perhaps after forty years in office, he would be assassinated. The public wrath . . .

"Here we are," the driver said.

Getting out, he knew that he would fight to see the hearings continued.

He was late. Already the other four Senators were seated. Bud nodded to them and took his place. He put his brief case (it gave him a sense of importance to carry one) on the table before him and unzipped it as if to be ready to delve into its contents to document his every statement.

The atmosphere was tense. Bud looked from face to face. Senator Stilson was granite hostility. Senator Gutenleigh avoided his eyes. Senator Klein glared at him truculently.

"It was called for eight," Senator Stilson said icily.

"Good evening, gentleman," he said. "Sorry I'm late."

"Good evening," Senator Rawlins said. "These gentlemen here," he included everyone but Bud in his gesture, "intend to dispense with a report and merely issue the Committee's recommendation. They've already decided to close the hearings and present the matter to the Senate tomorrow."

Bud was stunned. This was unbelievable. That meant . . . that . . . The friends! Somehow they had gotten to Gutenleigh, the Senator from Hawaii. Bud had counted on him—on the basis of his television vote—to oppose Klein and Stilson. What outrageous, Un-American pressure had been exerted to cause him to surrender?

"But . . . but . . . Senator Guten—"

"Has," Senator Stilson said in his thin, peevish tenor, "reconsidered."

Enmity and hostility flared silently from the Chairman. An almost baffled look crossed his face as if the implications had finally arrived in his consciousness: here was a Senator, Senator Council, a member of—as he thought of it—his *team,* who had had the temerity to transgress his leadership. One would expect opposition from a radical like Rawlins. But from a Council . . . ! He had always felt that Bud was one of his. The insult was compounded by heresy.

"I feel," Senator Rawlins said, "that two questions require further exploration: how is it that the starmen are so ignorant of basic scientific principles; and for what reason do they insist that we reach such a momentous decision in such a limited time? To ask the Senate to vote now would force an honest man to perhaps a hasty decision. For myself, until these points are clarified, I would be very reluctant to reach any sort of an agreement with them. I want to ask this Committee to reconsider its decision, and I hope the Honorable Senator from Missouri will join with me, and that between us we can prevail upon the other gentlemen."

A sincere democrat, he spoke with quiet desperation, "In order to expect the people to choose wisely, we must be sure that they are given an opportunity to receive all the pertinent facts."

Bud was howling inwardly with the fury of a thwarted child. Headlines were flying away from him. His stand in the full Senate would command only one one-hundredth of the attention it would receive here. He arose, trembling with rage.

Shaking a quivering finger at Senator Stilson he cried, "You have bribed Gutenleigh!"

Gutenleigh looked uncomfortable.

"What did they promise you, Sam?" he thundered, wondering wildly what counter promises he could make.

Even Senator Stilson was shocked by Bud's violent outburst. Bud was famous for his rabid thundering against subversives, but no one had expected him to have the courage to open such hysterical fire on his Senate colleagues. Senator Stilson said, "I resent your attitude, sir!"

"Gentlemen, Gentlemen," Senator Rawlins said. "A little moderation, please."

"I'm for them, damn you!" Bud cried. "You're all in a conspiracy—a filthy conspiracy—against me!"

"If you don't sit down, I will summon an officer and have you removed bodily from this Chamber," Senator Stilson said.

They were all looking at Bud. With a great display of reluctance, he sank to his seat. He refused to look at Senator Stilson. He sulked and plotted revenge. And remembered Frank and hated everybody.

The vote proceeded routinely. Three members voted to recommend that the Senate reject the starmen's offer. Senator Rawlins abstained, and Bud voted that the Senate accept it.

The committee meeting broke up. Senators Klein and

Stilson went out to gather up opposition Senators. They lobbied far into the night.

Nor was Bud to be outdone.

6

THE THREE spider ships waited in the late evening darkness. Only a few spectators loitered. The television cameras were quiet. Army sentries patroled the area to keep the starmen inside and the curious out. Norma's heels clicked sharply on the runway as she approached. At the ropes she stopped and showed the guard the entry permit her brother had obtained for her.

"Come under," the guard said, lifting the rope.

"The one called Herb?"

"He's in that one over there."

She moved in the indicated direction. A moment before, the night had been warm. Now an uncomfortably chill breeze whispered around her as she moved into the starship's shadow. The thought of the distance it had come, the countless millions of miles of space its hull had shed, was enough to dwarf her into less than insignificance. She wanted to run back to the guard, and to the protection of the familiar.

The ladder was down, and when she reached it, the door above opened and a starman looked out.

"I'd like to come up."

The starmen went away. In a moment, he was back with one of the three who could speak English.

"I'd like to come up," Norma repeated.

"We've already given the official tour for today."

"I have an authorization from our government. I'd like to talk to Herb. You tell him I'm from Senator Council. It's about the report."

"Just a moment." He disappeared inside. Norma teetered nervously back and forth. Wonderingly she put out her hand to touch the hard, icy metal of the ladder.

"Come up."

She began to climb toward the opening. Looking behind her, she saw Washington, real and solid and reassuring.

The starman at the top helped her inside.

Herb was coming down the narrow corridor. She smiled at him. "Hello."

"Hello . . ."

"I want to talk to you a moment."

He gestured her inside.

In the first room off the main corridor, Herb stopped. Several starmen hovered nearby to listen.

"Can I talk to you for just a couple of seconds alone?"

"Why—why, yes, I guess." He looked around for permission.

The Oligarch, towering imperiously on the fringe of the group, said, "Why don't you interview her in my office, Herb?"

"Come along," Herb said.

In contrast to the Spartan plainness of the rest of the ship, the Oligarch's office was richly furnished. Its private corridor led past the messhall and opened upon the main corridor that led forward to the second level: it was strategically located; from its doorway, one could interdict entrance and escape.

It was the first time Herb had been in the room. Automatically his eyes searched the walls.

"Senator Council asked me to talk to you," Norma said. "He wants you to understand about the report. You've heard? It's going to the full Senate tomorrow. We'd like you to . . ."

"I'm only a technician, Miss."

"My name is Norma."

"Norma." His emotions were tangled beyond solution. He wanted to say, 'I'll stay behind when the others leave, will that make everything all right, you won't blame me, you won't blame me for it if I stay behind, will you?' His mind hurt with the confusion.

"We thought, if you'd go away, if the people thought we'd actually lost you . . ."

"It's not for me to make any kind of decision. I'll have to ask. Would that be all right, sir?"

Norma blinked. She did not understand to whom the

question was addressed. Her eyes followed his to the wall, a concealed microphone? She felt a little prickle of fear.

The Oligarch stood in the doorway behind her. "That will be agreeable with us."

She whirled guiltily.

"Bud wanted to, to see Herb tonight . . ." Norma felt resentment against this man in the doorway. "I was told to bring Herb."

"I will be able to speak for my government."

"I was told to bring Herb," Norma said stubbornly. Bud had not specified, but she told herself that she would not yield to a stranger. She did not consider Herb a stranger. "Isn't it all right to take him?

"He may come, too, if you wish." He smiled. "Whatever you wish."

His voice was not reassuring. "Thank you." She modified her tone. Some of the iciness went out of it. "I'll leave now. Bud will send two C.I.A. men over for you."

Sitting at his desk in his Georgetown apartment, Bud looked through a stack of letters.

Norma, waiting, tried to become interested in a *Saturday Evening Post* story and failed. She put the magazine aside.

The knock they were waiting for came.

Bud rose and crossed quickly to the door.

"Ah, hello," he said with a genial smile. "If you gentlemen will wait downstairs, I'll call you when they are ready to leave." The C.I.A. men withdrew. "Hello, young fellow. Herb, I believe? And?"

"George . . . How would George be?"

"George," the Senator said, pumping the Oligarch's hand and drawing him across the threshold. "I like your people's way of using first names. Very democratic. Just call me Bud."

They arranged themselves around the room.

"I don't suppose you'd care for a drink?"

"I'd be delighted," George said.

Bud, solemn faced, mixed the drinks, talking over his shoulder. "I hope you haven't taken our Committee report as a rejection of your generous offer . . . You understand? I want to explain my position—what we, you and

I, can do . . . There we are." He turned from his labors and handed the drinks around.

"Norma, Herb. I wonder if you'd mind if George and I stepped in there?"

"It's all right with us," Norma said.

Bud and the Oligarch went into the study. Bud closed the door.

"Now," he said. Ambition was a sickness in him. *This is the boy I've got to sell,* he thought. That's all I've got to do: sell him. Once he's sold, the rest will follow. Ambition was like a hunger, and success hung in the air like smoke. "We can have a nice, private talk. I'm sure you'll appreciate my rather delicate position."

George swirled ice and smiled.

"Norma tells me you can speak for your government?"

George nodded.

"Let's sit down."

"Thank you."

"Now here's the way I feel about it. I'm on your team. We're both on the same team. I want to help you all I can, and I know you'll want to help me."

George nodded.

"I was thinking: if you would leave. Not tell anybody. Leave tonight. I don't mean for good, but make it look that way. You see?"

"Our leaving would serve as an emotional shock?"

"Yes, exactly. Your leaving might be just what the people need to wake them up and get them on our team. I don't need to tell you that the Senate is likely to reject your offer. I meant right now. The way things stand now. My first mail is coming in. It's predominantly unfavorable. But some telegrams I've gotten, I think the people are coming around. But they're still not around yet. We need a couple of weeks. My idea is, I'd like to be the one that —more or less—handles it."

"You want us to work through you?"

"You have put your finger on it, George. If there's just one Earthman you can trust and work through, who knows the ropes . . ."

"I believe I understand."

"And when you come back, you make it plain that it

was Bud Council who brought you back—it was Bud Council who really convinced you to return."

"You and I," George said, "will probably be able to work out a deal."

Jubilation rang in Bud's ears. This was it. The talk of working out a deal was an assurance of victory. President Bud—no, perhaps it would be better, more dignified, to be President *Phil.* He would write it out and see which looked best: President Philip Council or President Bud Council . . . History lay heavily upon his thoughts . . . For the first time he actually felt at home with a starman.

"Perhaps you would do something for us?" George said.

Bud found himself looking deep into George's eyes. Instinctively he knew that George knew him better than he knew himself, and that George had carefully studied him according to no one could tell what alien science.

"Why why, yes, yes, of course."

"Well," George said, rising and going to Bud and dropping a hand across his shoulder, "just to be sure that you really are on our team, perhaps you could give us a little token of loyalty."

Bud grew cold in anticipation. But the crowds cheering and the banners waving . . . No! Not now, they couldn't snatch it away now! What was it George wanted? Money? A signed agreement? Patronage? "Why, yes, naturally."

George's hand tightened in friendly reassurance. He knew that he had found his man. "Your brother's head. I believe his name is Frank. His head. We'll expect you to have it for us when we return in two weeks. Two weeks from tomorrow."

He no longer needed to count on Herb.

7

THE STARMEN had vanished into the night that is deepest just before dawn, when the sky is black and most mysterious. They had ordered the guards away, their lifts had whirled, they rose, and far above the Earth there were ruby tongues of jets and the volcanic roar of power.

The airport lay desolate.

. . . In his ship, Herb could not sleep. He kept reviewing the time he had spent alone with Norma. It was difficult to remember clearly. What few things he could remember would, he was afraid, be lost forever in the jungle of confusion that was his mind unless he went over them again and again and planted them firmly and deeply into his being.

What an alien and lovely name, Norma. Something about her was so quiet and reassuring. He wanted to bury his head against her breasts and whisper, "I wish I could save your planet, but I can't." He had wanted to confess to her, but he could not. If she had discovered . . . But now, in the darkness, on the narrow cot, he thought about her and buried his head against her soft breasts, and he smelled the cool darkness of the perfume, and he spoke to her and told her the truth, and she understood his hurt and knew the necessity and forgave him . . .

The trouble began one week after the take off. The Oligarch read well the signals of its arrival, but he did nothing. A scene would be bad for the crew's morale. He thought it would be a tonic to his own. It would prove the validity of his conclusion: that the indoctrinated starman called Leslie would crack up on the seventh day.

It happened, as he imagined it would, shortly after Leslie had filled out his dream form.

It was in the messhall.

Without warning Leslie kicked over his chair. His face twisted. His hands whitened at the knuckles. There was an insane expression in his eyes. He looked slowly around the table.

With his first movement there came silence; it was instantaneous; it was as though the clock had stopped in a parlor of corpses. No one moved.

He screamed a great, searing curse. The word was English.

The crew waited. No one breathed.

Leslie began to break things with mounting fury. He

shattered his plate by slamming it savagely to the table. He threw his cup against the far wall.

They waited. Many of them cried inward encouragement to insanity.

"Lies!" he screamed in English. "Lies! *There is no Universe!*"

He fell to his hands and knees and growled and snapped like an animal.

The Oligarch felt his detachment shatter. Hurriedly he left his table and went to Leslie and killed him.

Breathing with difficulty, he arose and addressed the crew. "This is what happens to a man who lies on his dream form." They rustled uneasily. "Go back to your meal."

One by one they resumed eating. Slowly conversation grew and expanded from whispers to abnormal loudness and then back to whispers again. The ubiquitous microphones peered up eagerly from the tables and the hungry record tapes consumed the sounds.

The food lodged in Herb's throat. There seemed no moisture anywhere in his body. He fought down an irrational impulse to get to his own feet and scream forever.

Once again at his private table, the Oligarch was amazed to find that the complete justification of his own logic left him feeling empty and unsatisfied and disappointed. The matter was behind him. In the future could he expect equal success? Insatiable doubt grew.

He stood up. The compulsion to wash his hands was irresistible. He left the mess hall hurriedly.

As he watched the cool cleanness of the water flow over his hands, he felt at peace.

He was a god, playing with men, knowing them as they would never know themselves, seeing into their inmost souls, moving them to his will.

He was tempted to greater accomplishment. Could he —could he—? Unsure of himself, he was doomed to seek endless reassurance.

Herb. Now Herb. There was a dangerous man. At least, he would become one, in another three days. It would be like playing with fire to play with Herb. It would be exciting, too.

He dried his hands. His heart was beating faster.

Herb would soon begin to doubt. William was already doubting. He should have done something about them both before now. About Leslie before now . . .

I will see that Herb . . . that Herb . . . what?

His mouth was dry. Excitement swelled and made his breath catch. His throat ached.

He would help William to doubt. None of them must return to Brionimar.

It was intensely rewarding to play God, if you could get your hands clean.

The Oligarch rang the buzzer. He would leave the mike tapes and the dream forms until this afternoon.

He would interview William now.

He was washing his hands when William entered.

After the interview, William came in and sat on Herb's cot.

In recent days, their common knowledge had drawn them together; before, they had scarcely spoken. Whenever they talked now, they used English, partly as a recognition of their kindred uniqueness, partly as a futile subconscious attempt to outwit the spy tapes.

"It's a ridiculous planet," Herb said.

"Yes, a ridiculous planet," William agreed.

"Freedom," Herb said. "That is nonsense."

"Equality," William said. "Equality. They are down right silly."

"You wouldn't think a place like that could exist, a silly place like that, where a man can actually say whatever silly idea pops into his mind."

"Yes," William said. "They should be destroyed—even if it wasn't necessary, they should be destroyed."

Herb was silent for a moment. The microphones listened. Then: "Imagine how awful it would be to live down there, with no one to do your thinking for you."

"The natural leaders aren't even recognized. You can't tell an Oligarch from a Subject."

"I'd never like to live in a place like that," Herb said. *I dreamed of it,* he wanted to say, *and I dreamed that Brionimar had been changed into Earth, and there was no Oli-*

garchy, and a man was free. "It's like a nightmare," he said.
They fell silent.

William wanted to say: *If only we could take that dream back with us, if only our people could see.*

"Yes," Herb said suddenly. "God, yes, yes."

"Eh?"

". . . nothing."

"He called me in today," William said.

"Oh?"

"We talked."

"What did you talk about?"

"Not much . . . I don't see what he was trying to get at." William stood up. He looked at the microphone. He felt courage grow in him. "I've been . . . *thinking* . . ."

Herb nodded. He dared not speak.

"You know what I mean?"

Herb nodded.

"We'll talk later."

After the fourth daily meal, William came once more. He took Herb's arm and gestured with his head that Herb should follow. Herb arose; his heart stood wildly beating in the cage of his chest; his blood ran with conspiracy and excitement.

They walked down the corridor until they were in a section free of microphones. It was, although they did not know it, intentionally unwired. It provided the crew a harmless escape valve for their emotions. It was not (as any Oligarch could have told you) necessary to watch a Subject all the time. Most of the spy tapes, as a matter of fact, were never even inspected.

William was sweating. Herb could not account for the intensity of emotional strain he seemed to be under. Herb imagined they would talk briefly—and plan vaguely—about ways to carry some of the idea and the feel of freedom back to Brionimar. They would bear a message of hope, they would tell that Earth had not been destroyed in vain, that a civilization could function in freedom without chaos. And perhaps, someday, not in their time, but someday . . .

"It's not perfect," Herb said. "We dream of perfection,

do you understand, but even Earth is not perfect. I think we ought to remember that. I can feel it, I can tell it. I . . . We want to take that back with us, too."

William was scarcely listening. His muscles were tense and crawling with danger. He had to speak, to confide, to know that he was not alone. To have Herb help him. Herb, too, must know.

"Listen," he hissed. "You know what I meant when I said I've been thinking?"

"Yes," Herb said. "So have I."

William licked his lips. His heart seemed to stop. He took a deep breath.

"How can we stop him from blowing it up?"

The Universe wheeled. Herb could not believe what he had heard. A Destructionist!

"He dropped some hints, he didn't mean to, but he did," William said. "I finally realized. You must have known longer than I have. It's all a lie. He as good as told me so."

Herb took half a step backward. His skin crawled with horror.

William, oblivious to everything but his own words, said, "We've got to stop and plan carefully. I will kill him myself, and then you get to the control room . . . We'll have to hold the crew off. They might not believe us. Not at first. That will be the big trouble . . ."

Herb continued to back away. All the training of a lifetime surged into his mind. There is scarcely a way to express the detestation a starman, properly conditioned felt toward a Destructionist. His reason was destroyed. He wanted to leap at William and tear at his face with his naked hands.

I've got to warn *him!* Herb thought.

He turned and ran. The Oligarch! I've got to warn him! Breath sobbed in his throat.

William watched the fleeing figure. He reached out a hand to stay him. He could not believe his own miscalculation. He stood, limp and defeated. There was no will left in him. Bleak betrayal was a heavy winged vampire.

There was no place to go.

He sat down.

It was all very logical for the first time in his life. Somewhere in time the Oligarchy had invented the menace as a device to gain (or to retain) power. They had saturated the people with ignorance, ridiculed thought, and eliminated freedom until the menace could not be challenged. They had established a closed and consistent system that could justify anything. And now that he had gotten outside, stepped beyond it, by denying its ultimate premise, the immensity of the fraud was mind staggering. There was no combating it as long as one lived inside. There have, he thought, been other Earths. Nothing outside the system must be permitted to intrude.

He put his head in his arms and began to cry.

That was how they found him when they came to kill him.

Herb did not watch the kill. He went straight to his cot and lay down and waited for the news to come. He heard the rustle of voices in the corridor as the hunt was being organized.

He was still trembling with disgust: a Destructionist! The very word sent a shudder through his body. To think that William, of them all, that William, would have been one seemed impossible. Still, you could never tell. A neighbor, a friend . . . You could never tell who might be.

How could they think? What sort of creatures could they be? Herb's imagination shrank from the task. It was one thing to hate the Oligarchy, but it was quite another to favor the end of the Universe.

The rustle of voices diminished. They were after him. They would get him.

Herb thought: Perhaps with this one action I have saved the Universe. When this becomes known on Brionimar, when it is learned how I, single handed, exposed the menace, then they will . . .

But suppose William was right?

Never before had such a thought even fought for recognition, and now, without warning, it erupted in naked completeness. It was an electric shock.

No! he shrieked, *no!*

He was sitting erect. He was clammy with icy perspiration. His whole body was suddenly silent and listening, every muscle and nerve strained in the direction of the hunt.

He lay back.

No, he thought.

The next day the Oligarch called him in.

"I want to thank you again, Herb." He watched his words sink into naked flesh. "If you had not told me, I would never have suspected. But for you, he—he might have succeeded."

Herb refused to look into the Oligarch's face. I did right, he thought. I did what I had to do, what anyone would have done.

"I know it has been a shock," the Oligarch said. "You were very fond of William."

Herb's lips twisted silently.

"I want to tell you a story," the Oligarch said. "Listen, listen carefully. It is about a man called Bud and what he did."

Herb was not listening; and then suddenly he was listening. The Oligarch told the story, and when he was done, leaned forward, waiting. It was as if Herb had just heard the most important story in the world.

"His brother's head," the Oligarch whispered, "he traded his brother's head for power . . ."

There was something about the idea that reached deep into the ancient folk shadows of Herb's mind and stood as a symbol. But he did not understand about symbols: only their compulsive effects. All his rage and frustration and guilt crystalized around Bud. If he could only see Bud fall and gasp and die, he would have vindicated morality and done all that he could do in the name and cause of justice.

"You may go," the Oligarch said. "Think about what I've told you."

8

Norma missed Herb. There was the glamor of the unknown about him and the appeal of the familiar. He was two individuals, a little boy, confused and puzzled and mute and needing her, and a man, strong and wise and belonging to a strange world she could not enter as she had entered all too easily the masculine world of Earth.

She was with Frank when Bud made his television announcement.

Bud beamed happily in the glare of uncounted millions of dollars of publicity. "At my invitation," he said, "the starmen have consented to return."

Frank winced to see what he thought to be a decent cause advancing the personal fortunes of a fool, a hypocrite, and a coward.

Bud—it was a little difficult to imagine (without having heard it) how he managed it—at the high point of his speech inserted a few remarks about home, mother, and the virtues of honesty and hard work. He was, he explained, a poor but honest man, holding certain principles dear to his heart. He was at a loss to account for the fact that he had been chosen to lead this great crusade for the starmen. "We can thank Almighty God that they have consented to return. *They will return.* I do not believe there are enough Communists in the country today to prevent it."

Frank shuddered to think what might happen now. Suppose Bud should—God, no!—become President out of all this; suppose the people, in gratitude, or the politicians seeking a popular hero, contrived his election.

Frank felt that he might have erred in using bad means to gain good ends. For Bud, hunting subversives, socialists, liberals, and critics, could rapidly reduce the country to conformism and with native ingenuity, pervert starscience into a political weapon.

135

The first radio message, on Earth frequency, to the President requested that Bud be given the job of handling all negotiations. If, it said, Senator Council finds it in his heart to accept the responsibility.

Many people did not understand the last.

Bud did.

The morning of the day the starmen returned, Norma came into Bud's office. She was practically bursting with excitement. Thoughts of what their knowledge would contribute to Earth, the marvelous advances in medicine, in physics, in art that hovered just within reach . . .

On her way through the secretary's office, she passed a slight, nattily dressed man wearing a hat.

For a puzzled second she furrowed her brow. Then memory came. He had been investigated by the Senate Crime Committee. She bit her lip in exasperation. Why would Bud be willing to see someone like that?

"Wasn't that—?" she demanded, bursting into Bud's office.

He got up with quick awkwardness. His face was bloodless. "Ohhhhhh," he sighed. "I didn't expect—Hello, Sis."

"Wasn't that—?" she began again.

"It's, it's, it's, he, he . . ." Bud indicated the box on his desk. "From an old friend."

"What's wrong? Don't you feel well, Bud?"

"Fine, fine," Bud said. "I feel fine . . . I'm very busy just now."

Norma sat down. The box rested on the desk between them. Warily Bud sank into his chair. She saw his face framed above the box, almost as if the head were hanging suspended and bodiless, and she felt an unaccountable tremor of superstitious fear.

"You poor dear," she said. "You've been worrying so much about the starmen . . . You're losing weight. Have Frank give you a checkup, Bud; you ought to take things easier."

". . . I will. I've been intending to . . . I'll have him look me over. Where is he; do you know where he is?"

"He went out last night. I expect him back any time."

He stood up. He was calmer now. He rested one hand

on the box. "Yes, I wouldn't worry. He'll show up. I am tired, terribly tired. You saw the Secret Service men out there? They're out to kill me, Norma! *Senator Stilson is hiring them!*"

Norma started to protest.

"I tell you, they are. If the Secret Service weren't out there to protect me, I'd be dead right now. But God has given me a job to do. I can't let them kill me until I have done His will."

"Bud, you're just overworked. Nobody's trying to do a thing like that. Frank says it's just publicity, and I thought . . ."

"Ahhhhh," Bud said darkly. "Would the President have assigned me a body guard if it weren't true? *Would he?* There are extremists in this country—Communists and Socialists—who stop at nothing to prevent the starmen from coming back. Even Frank . . ."

Norma's face grew a shade paler. "But he's the one . . ."

"You can never tell! But I'll tell you this. I pray every night, Sis. I get down on my knees, and I pray that God will let me live long enough." Bud's mind suddenly flashed back to his childhood, and he remembered praying that God would let him assassinate Stalin. God needed only to arm him and transport him to the Kremlin. He could have done the rest. He shook his head darkly again. "You don't understand the dangers." He felt courageous. It took *guts* to face the Communist menace.

She wanted to run. She clenched her fists. This is Bud, your brother, she thought. He's just upset. "I just wanted to see you for a moment," she said. "It wasn't about anything important."

Bud rubbed his hand caressingly over the box. "Yes?"

"I'll let you get back to work."

She stood up and started for the door.

"Don't worry about Frank!" Bud said sharply. "He's all right. Nothing's happened to him."

Norma was gone.

Bud began to cry, and looking at the box, he whispered, "It's all your fault. You made me do it. You did, *you made me!*"

HERB KNEW, even before the spider ships touched ground, that he was going to murder Bud.

The ships were motionless. Slowly suspense mounted. At last one ship opened its port. The landing ladder spun away.

Down came the Oligarch, alone, dressed simply in a solid color double breasted suit. A businessman's suit. There was something reassuring and normal about him. There was initial silence, and then the cheer rose and thundered.

He went directly to the platform. President Wilkerson advanced to meet him. Their hands joined, and a pleasantry passed unheard beneath the cheering. The Oligarch surveyed the welcoming party of Congressmen, foreign diplomats, and government officials. He saw Bud. He crossed to him.

The cheer became deafening.

They exchanged a few whispered words. Lip readers might have caught the question and the assent. Then, smiling, they turned to the public. Nodding, waving, Bud (visibly upset about something) tried to give the impression of recognizing each face individually. The Oligarch bowed his head modestly.

Herb watched from the port of the spider ship. He clenched his fists angrily. If only he had a weapon of some sort.

The President spoke briefly.

Then, as the Oligarch moved toward the speaker's platform, Herb dropped swiftly down the ladder. His feet touched the ground.

The Oligarch watched from the corner of his eye. Herb moved toward the crowd. The crowd leaned forward to catch the Oligarch's every word.

And he was cleansed. He was free of all responsibility: it was now between Herb and Bud. If Herb succeeded . . .

"Ladies and gentlemen," he began.

They were hushed.

"Thank you for your reception. I stand today before . . ." His voice translated into a billion volts, blanketed the world with supersonic vibrations made audible by
millions of loudspeakers.

He needed pay no attention to his speech. His mind was
floating free, and his body was light and youthful. There
were only a few more things to be done, and then his role
would be finished.

"On this momentous occasion," the Oligarch continued.

Herb was free of the worst of the crowd. He resisted
an impulse to run. He, too, was wearing a businessman's
suit. It was the same one he had worn for the hearings.
In it, he was indistinguishable from an Earthman. He
pulled his hat lower over his face and pushed his way outward. Faces turned, eyes alerted with curiosity, shoulders
shrugged, faces turned away. Herb did not know that
Norma had seen him and was now trying to fight her way
free of humanity to follow him.

The Oligarch continued his speech. His grim and gloomy
reflections vanished. He peered out at the Earth faces
with genuine benevolence. *It's not in my hands any longer,*
he wanted to tell them. *One of your Senators will make the
ultimate decision, unless one of my starmen kills him first.*

And then inwardly he chuckled. Or perhaps, he could
have said, *my starman will experience some incident, perhaps even a trivial one, that will awaken him to the fact
that the universe is not in danger. In which event, he will
not be able to convince you of the danger to Earth. For
in due time, I will announce his escape as a dangerous
lunatic.*

Herb's feet moved rhythmically against the sidewalk.
For one moment, there was a sense of freedom and im-
pending loss. No more dream forms, his feet seemed to
echo.

No

more

dream

forms . . .

And coloring it, the perception of the world around him, the bright air, the hot sun, the colors and the gentle wind. Perhaps the colors were most startling, for on Brionimar there was universal drabness that approached decay. The Oligarchy struck out at all frivolity, sensing danger to itself in all sensuous pleasure.

And then the beauty, the sheer, heart-stopping beauty of freedom and color burst on him; his conditioning collapsed. Earth knowledge surged across his memories.

It must not die, he thought, forgetting hatred in beauty. It must not, because there is so much that is good, that is noble, that is sad and mighty . . .

"Hello," Norma said breathlessly.

He whirled. For an instant he was terrified. He saw that she was alone.

He relaxed. Warmth grew within him. "Hello." Until now, it had not occurred to him that he might have been followed.

"Why did you—?"

A radio was blaring somewhere, and as he looked at her, both of them half laughing, they both heard the announcement that would be headlined shortly in the papers, as:

RENEGADE STARMAN ESCAPES SHIP. FEAR INSANE, SAYS GEORGE.

EARTH AUTHORITIES ALERTED. (Full description of escapee on page two.)

THIS MAN IS ARMED AND DANGEROUS.

10

HERB HUNCHED his shoulders as if to ward off a suspected blow. Norma's eyes mirrored fright and uncertainty, and she moved half a step from him.

Grasping her arm at the elbow, he said, "We have to get off the streets."

Norma wanted to twist away from him and run.

"You've got to help me hide!" The pressure seemed threatening.

"Let me go!"

He dropped his hand instantly. "You've got to help me."

From the expression on his face, she knew that she had nothing to fear. She felt ashamed of herself.

"We can go to my hotel," she said.

Once in the hotel, Herb's eyes darted around the four walls of the living room.

"There are no microphones," Norma said.

They stood just inside the door. Norma turned and walked decisively to the divan. She sat down. "I think you'd better explain."

"I . . . I need some money," Herb said. "There's something I have to get."

"What is it?"

"I . . . Pleast trust me, *please,*" he said.

She hesitated; then: "How much do you need?"

"A . . . hundred dollars. Could you let me have—loan me—that much?"

Norma knew he was not insane; there was something here that she did not understand, but it was not insanity. Her emotions went out to him. She saw the present situation only in personal terms, their own relationship. She saw no wider implications. Intuition, she would have called it. Decisively, she phoned for the bellboy and when he came, gave him a check for the management to cash.

While they were waiting for the money, she said, "Won't you tell me—?"

"I can't. I can't. I wish I could. Please, if you'll—" he hesitated, and then, with sickness and loathing, said, "trust me . . ."

The money came.

"I'll try to pay you back; make it up to you some way . . ."

"That's all right. Where are you going? What are you going to buy?"

Perhaps it was the desire to shock her, to destroy her faith in him, perhaps and more probably, it was the need to confess (and hope for absolution) that he said: "I want to buy a gun."

"Why do you want a gun?"

Herb, still standing, tried to memorize her face. He was acutely aware of his isolation. He wanted to go to her side, to talk rapidly, to reveal the cruel and horrible compulsion that was driving him—and most of all, to enlist her aid and her understanding. He needed to know that one single individual in the whole Universe could appreciate his attempt to meet his own standard of truth and morality.

"Tell me. Maybe Bud will be able to help you out of your trouble . . . He's my brother . . ."

The complexity of emotions that burst upon him was almost impossible to understand. He had thought of her —if he had actually thought of the connection at all— as an employee of Bud's, perhaps, but no more than that. He asked incredulously: "Frank was your brother?"

"You mean . . . is my brother?"

"Yes . . . I, yes, of course."

"What did you mean: was my brother?" Uneasiness settled deep inside her. "Has something happened to him?"

"No. No. It was a grammatical error." Herb thought the sentence too stiff for credence. But she seemed reassured.

"I'll get Bud to help you. And Frank, too. Perhaps the three of us can get you out of any trouble you're in. I'm sure the starmen will be fair. If it's something you've done . . ."

"No! Don't talk to Bud! Don't tell him you've seen me. You mustn't!"

"Herb, you're being silly." She stood up. "You make it sound like I've got something to be afraid of from my own brother."

Herb bit his lips in anguish and ran from the room.

Norma heard his feet on the carpet, running, running . . .

The empty room became a thing of terror. She was entangled in something beyond her understanding, and the world seemed less secure than at any time since her parents had died. Should she go after Herb, or . . . ?

She started toward the telephone, stopped, turned away —and then turned back.

She got the switchboard.

"Get me Senator Council's office . . . Hello, oh, hello, John. Norma. Is Bud in yet? Oh, still. Have him call me as soon as he—oh. All right. I'll be over in an hour then. And John: have you heard anything from Frank? I'm beginning to get worried about him. He isn't in yet . . ."

She hung up slowly, wondering if she had done the proper thing.

She was early for the appointment with Bud, and she was waiting in the outer office when he came in. His two guards nodded recognition and Bud said, "What is it, Norma?" His tone was irritable, and she wanted to cry.

"Please, may I talk to you a minute?"

Bud shifted his weight nervously.

"Please, Bud!"

"Come on. I haven't got all day." Letting her enter the main office before him, he said, "What's it about this time?"

He drew the door to his private office closed after them, and went to his desk where he picked up a letter and pretended to read it. "Well? Well?"

"I've talked to Herb."

Bud's face sagged. The letter began to tremble ever so slightly. Norma did not notice. He did not look up. How much did Herb know? About Frank? Did he know? "Yes?"

He felt weakness dissolve his arm muscles and dissolve the muscles of his thighs and calves. He was afraid that he was about to suffer a heart attack. He had difficulty breathing. "What—what did he have to say?"

"He wanted me to buy a gun for him."

"What for? What for? What did he want a gun for?"

Norma twisted her hands nervously. "I don't know. He wouldn't say. He's in trouble. I thought maybe we could help him."

"He didn't say anything else?" Bud demanded sharply, feeling the fear fade. "He didn't tell you, he didn't say anything else?"

"No, just that he needed a gun—"

"Where is he now?"

"I don't know."

"You don't know? You don't know? He's trying to get a gun, and you don't know where he is?"

"I—I—"

"No telling what kind of a crazy fool idea he's got. No telling what kind of lies he'd tell about me!"

"He's in trouble, Bud. We ought to—"

"You listen to me! You do what I say! Don't pay any attention to anything he says. If you see him again, you call me!"

"I think I'd better talk to Frank about it, Bud. Have you seen him?"

Bud was on his feet and around the desk. He grabbed her shoulders and began to shake her. Her face drained of color. His nostrils flared white.

"Bud! Bud! What's got into you?"

"Frank's all right!" Bud cried. "Now, get out, get out, GET OUT!" He shoved her away from him. "Get out," he sobbed.

Half dazed, she backed away, opened the door, and disappeared.

Trembling, Bud sank into his chair. It was a long time before his breathing returned to normal. He counted his pulse with intent concentration, feeling it flutter like a wounded bird beneath his finger tips.

11

HERB HAD no real hope of eluding capture. After he fled from Norma, he pulled his hat low over his face and hurried down the street. At the first hotel, he entered and registered and was shown his room.

He fell on the bed; the room was fuzzy and dull. He wanted nothing more than to sleep. His mind was such a searing agony of doubt that he had to escape from it. He curled up warmly and nestled against the softness of the mattress and closed his eyes, trying to drive all thought from him, and he slept . . .

When he awoke, the room was heavy with darkness and silence, and he lay still, trying to feel the vibration of the ship's motors. The memory of a formless dream clung to his mind, and he tried to clarify it for the dream form.

Awareness of his location came. He relaxed, wanted to sleep again, thought: no more dream forms, no more . . . Other memories stirred and returned, and he was uneasily awake. He opened his eyes, growing tense.

He held his breath. The dark around him concealed unknown dangers. He was still fully clothed, and he stood up. He found the light switch.

With the bright flame of electricity he became aware of how heavy his head was; how incoherent his thoughts were; and there was a sour taste in his mouth. He blinked his eyes. The room was reassuringly normal.

He went back to bed and lay down. His thoughts whirled. Beyond thought there was a great, tugging emptiness in his stomach, a sense of despair that semed to dwell in every tiny muscle and radiate outward from every tiny blood vessel. The light made him naked, and he could not face his own nakedness.

He turned out the light and returned to the bed. The dark was protective and reassuring now, and he closed his eyes.

Bit by bit the sense of unreality fled.

Dawn came.

The TV set sat squatly on the table across the room. Morning sunshine fell brightly through the Venetian blinds. Herb turned on the set to discover the latest news of his pursuit.

The screen lighted and on its surface formed the deadly trinity of the starships. It was a long shot from a sound truck, and the camera panned an expanse of desert beyond to focus briefly on the Arizona sunrise.

An announcer was commenting on the riot of color that was quite obvious to the viewer: the flame of dawn in the sky and the blood red of the prairie flowers that covered the desert.

Herb watched and listened.

The starships were in place. Their cutting beams lanced

out, there were puffs of destruction, and the tubings struck into the ground.

The camera near one of the ships observed the operation intently. A scientist was commenting on the technology of the starmen. "The information inherent in one of these ships alone," he said (characteristically underestimating the pace of advancement), "would be enough to thrust Earth a hundred years—in terms of scientific knowledge —into the future."

A shudder spun through Herb's body. He paced the room restlessly. Somewhere at a distance a clock struck the hour. Outside the open window, English sparrows chattered shrill, imperative commands.

Herb was hungry. He phoned the desk and ordered breakfast. He was in the bath room when the bellboy arrived; he called, "The money's on the dresser." For fear of being recognized, he remained hidden until the bellboy left.

He came out. The tray was on the night table. Eating, he continued to watch the progress of the starships.

The voice of the Oligarch now came from the TV. He fabricated plausible details about what they were discovering of Earth's early physical history.

Sweaty faces advanced and receded from the cameras. The three tubes continued into the Earth, going deeper by the minute.

A sense of urgency and desperation filled Herb. He must hurry to kill Bud. By noon the desert operation would be completed. Earth would be a mined planet. Destruction could then be accomplished by the flick of a switch.

He looked at his face in the mirror. Black stubble pricked his skin in a thousand places, and he ran his hand across his cheek. He shrugged and found his hat.

Until sunset, he told himself, he would have until sunset to accomplish his self-imposed assignment.

Bud, he thought (and revulsion mounted in him), is her brother, and she, his sister; and Frank, Frank is dead and forgotten and hidden somewhere, as soon will be now the Earth and all its beauty.

He was in the street. The sunshine was bright. He walked.

A gun, he thought, for a hand that is hungry for—and he thought: To cup the hand behind Norma's head, and stroke her hair, and look deeply into her eyes. He looked at his hands; strange, hungry hands, he thought. He felt them tighten against the metallic iciness of a gun . . .

"You can't," the man behind the counter said, "buy a pistol without a permit. You'll have to get a police permit before I can sell you a gun." His eyes shifted uneasily from Herb's face, and Herb thanked the man and started back toward the sunshine.

"Wait a minute!" the man said.

The harsh command froze Herb. He turned. He found himself looking into reward-hungry eyes. The hand below them held an automatic. The hand was trembling with greed.

"You're that starman," the proprietor said.

Herb caught his breath. He jerked to his left and spun around. He ran.

The harsh roar of the automatic burst behind him. The proprietor had taken flight for an admission of identity; but perhaps latent uncertainty had carried the bullet high. It smashed into the window pane above Herb's head, and glass fragments erupted upon the pavement.

"Stop him! Stop him!" cried the proprietor as Herb fled.

The sunlight was bright. Herb bolted across an intersection, narrowly missed being run down by a car, dodged around a heavy truck and ran to the left.

There was no more shooting. There was a hub-hub behind him. A policeman's whistle sounded.

Herb jerked around another corner. There was the sound of pursuit.

He ran a block, doubled back, entered a department store, lost himself in the crowd, took the elevator up to the third floor.

He tried to look interested in the merchandise. Each second cost him an extra heart beat. He left a counter and went to the stairs. He became inconspicuously preoccupied with distant thoughts. He was once more on the ground floor. He left the building by the opposite entrance.

He hailed a taxi. His heart beat desperately.

Once settled in the rear seat, he felt almost secure. The worst was over. He told the driver, "Down town."

After a dozen blocks, he got out. When the cab was gone, he walked back the way he had come. He found a hotel, registered, and was shown his room.

He stood at the window. A police car cruised by. For a moment, he was afraid it would stop.

I must get a gun, he thought. Time seemed to be falling swiftly in the bright air.

I must, I must.

He went to the television set and switched it on.

The starships were still occupying the screen. The sun was slanting it rays across the desert.

An announcer spoke in a dryly excited voice.

Herb sat down, and when at length one starship lumbered into the center of the triangle and its beam struck out, weariness and futility possessed him. They were planting the atomic seed. Within an hour there would be no hope of reprieve. There was none now; and yet it seemed, doom was not irreversible until this last act was accomplished and the seed in place.

Herb spun the selector. He did not want to witness the climactic moment.

What was the name of Norma's hotel?

He remembered.

He went to the telephone . . .

When Norma arrived in answer to the call, she found an unshaven Herb nervously pacing the floor.

"Where have you been?" she asked breathlessly.

He seated himself on the bed and wrinkled the coverlet in his hands, working with it furiously.

"They're going to blow up the world," he said.

"Who—What?"

"I helped them. It's my fault. I was a fool. I couldn't know, you see that? I couldn't *know* . . ."

Norma was ashen.

Herb stood up and crossed to her side and looked down at her. "Out in the desert, they have just finished planting the charge. That's what they came here for. They're going to blow up the world."

"The starmen?"

"Yes."

Norma was on her feet. She was too terrified to ask why. She did not question . . . *It was true!*

"We've got to stop them!"

"We can't, it's too late," Herb said.

"Why not, why is it?"

"It's too late."

"We've got to stop them."

"It's too late. There's nothing we can do. Listen. Get me a gun. I want to—"

He loomed wild-eyed above her. She didn't understand what he intended to do: only that some impossible fury was driving him. "You've got to help me stop them. There must be some way."

"Get me a gun! Get me a gun!" Every atom of his being cried out to her: he had to have the gun. His thoughts were warped and twisted. With the gun everything would be clear in his mind. Everything would follow step by step. The gun could spout a great, purifying flame.

He was alone in the room. He looked down. She had dropped her purse, and it had spilled open. He walked to the gun that had fallen from it.

Norma ran, wild and terrified. To whom could she turn? Frank! Where was he?

Frank . . .

Bud?

No. No, not Bud. He—

There was no one else. Bud. Her breath was fire. He would have to do something. Bud.

She hailed a cab.

"Bud!" she called as she opened the car door. "The Senate Office Building! Hurry!" Bud, she sobbed under her breath. He can do something to stop it.

Herb examined the gun carefully. He weighed it in his hand. It would do nicely. He pocketed it.

He would need only an instant. A taxi from here to the Senator's office. A trip in the elevator. Perhaps a slight wait: and then Senator Council framed in the doorway. He had—how long? Several hours, he told himself.

He touched the gun again. No hurry. No real hurry. Several hours.

Norma was hysterical when she burst into Bud's office. One of Bud's hands darted for the drawer where he had taken to keeping an automatic. The hand stopped.

Norma's lips were trembling uncontrollably. "Bud!" she gasped. *"Bud, they're planning to blow up the world!"*

"What are you talking about?" he demanded angrily. "What do you mean?"

"The starmen! I saw Herb. He told me. I had to come to you, Bud. You've got to make them stop it!"

"Nonsense," Bud said. "You're out of your mind. You're crazy." He surged to his feet. "Where is Herb? I told you to come see me if you found him. Where is he?"

"It's true!" Norma cried. "I know it's true! They've been lying to us. They spy on each other. They have hidden microphones everywhere. They want to destroy the world, Bud! Oh, please, please, please, you've got to believe me . . ."

Bud came toward her. She was insane, of course. It was astonishing how many people were insane. Sometimes Bud thought he was the only sane person left. "Now, now, you just tell me where Herb is, and I'll go have a nice long talk with him." He pocketed the automatic.

"You don't believe me."

"Oh, I do. Dear, I do, of course, I do. They're going to blow up the world . . . I'd like to see Herb and talk it over with him." He made soothing motions with his hands.

Bud's face, round and smiling and vacant, peered down. She wanted to throw something at it. She wanted to launch herself upon him and shake him and make him listen to her. He was a monolithic caricature of stupidity. She had to force herself into his mind and make him *see*.

Bud came no closer to her. "Now, now, everything's going to be all right," he said. "Now, now, brother's little sister is . . ." He took a half step backward.

She was able to see him for the first time as Frank saw him. A little sense of horror was born and began to grow.

She stared at him with slowly vanishing disbelief. How could someone like this be her brother? He was some cold, unfeeling, insensitive thing, wrapped up in a world that embraced no one but himself.

"What have you done to Frank?" she demanded. "Bud, *what have you done to my brother?*"

Bud half snarled.

And the Oligarch stepped out of the little room to the left. "I think it's about time I take over."

Norma felt her heart pulse and stop cold. Ice filled the air.

Bud said, staring at her with fascination, "She's going crazy, George."

Norma turned to the Oligarch. "What did you make him do to Frank?"

"Not here," Bud said softly. "Don't kill her yet. She knows where Herb is."

Norma wanted to scream. She only half opened her mouth when the Oligarch's hand slapped sharply against her neck. Her knees buckled and she dropped unconscious to the heavy carpet.

"She knows where Herb is," Bud said again. "We've got to find him before he tells someone—tells someone else about Frank."

"She was telling the truth," the Oligarch said. "We are going to blow up the world. That's what I came back to Washington to tell you."

Herb arrived at the new Senate Office Building. He paid his fare and dismissed the cab. No one noticed him as he entered the lobby. He took the elevator to Senator Council's office. He was taking his time; he had several hours.

The secretary, John, was behind his desk. The reception room was empty. Herb felt his stomach muscles tighten, and his hands clenched the pocketed gun tightly and grew damp.

"Yes?"

"I want to see the Senator."

"What is the nature of your business?"

"I want to talk about, about some private matters. I

can wait until he can see me." Herb felt the gun, heavy and reassuring.

"The Senator isn't in right now. Perhaps I can help you?"

"No," Herb said sharply. "My business is with him. It's just between the two of us."

"He just left with his sister and George, the starman."

Herb bent forward intently. Time telescoped. An hour was no longer a practical infinity. "Where did they go?"

"I don't know, sir."

To the spider ship, Herb thought. They came back to Washington. They came back—to give Bud his reward for betrayal . . .

Herb was at the door. He almost tore it from the hinges when he jerked it open.

John picked up his telephone and placed a call to the C.I.A "The starman, Herb," he said, "has just left Senator Council's office. You can pick him up outside. If you hurry."

Bud dismissed his bodyguard, and he and George supported Norma between them as they left the building by private elevator and subway to the garage. Bud's face was grey, his lips bloodless.

The Oligarch had presented him with a choice. Tomorrow morning, some high government official would receive in the mail Frank's head, along with Bud's signed confession. If Bud did not, before then, speak the key words that would blow up the planet. Bud, in the first stunned instant, cried: "Take me with you!" But even as he spoke, he knew that he was doomed. Knowledge did not prevent appeal, but it helped develop resignation. Bud thrust out with entreaties and debased himself with cowardly promises, and seeing them fail, tried threats which failed equally. His mind splintered into a thousand shards and reality became abstracted fragments of himself: the world ceased then to exist for him, and he lived in a phantom land, and his ego seized upon icebergs that drifted across the chill sea of thought.

He became noble.

Norma came to consciousness as the car, driven inexpertly by the Senator, rolled toward the airport. Early afternoon sunlight slanted down across the Capitol.

She lay very quiet in the back seat, listening to the hiss of the tires. Her neck was swollen and throbbing. *Don't kill her yet,* her own brother had said, and then, out of the silence of the car, came his own voice again, contradicting what had gone before.

"Dearer to me than all gold," Bud said. "Child of my beloved mother."

"We will take her with us," the starman answered soothingly, reassuringly.

"She's all that's left," Bud said.

Norma lay quiet, unmoving, not daring to open her eyes.

"You can't know what she means to me," Bud said. "You must tell her that. You must promise to tell her."

"I will do it. I promise you."

Bud said intently, "You must promise, I must know."

"I promise."

"Nothing will happen to her? She's all I have left. All. Child of my beloved mother."

Tension accumulated between Bud and the starman. Norma realized that her brother was no longer sane.

The car slowed and stopped. Still Norma did not move. She was too terrified. They came to her door and opened it.

George pulled her roughly from the seat. She moaned but she did not open her eyes. His hard muscles against her were deadly and threatening, and her knees were so weak that, had she wanted to, she could not have supported herself.

She heard a starman's feet on the steel ladder that descended from the spider ship. She felt herself scooped up and dropped over his shoulder. In the background she heard her brother's voice, "Child of . . ." The agony of the voice was almost unendurable. "You must tell her what I did to save her."

And she was jolted harshly upon the starman's shoulder as he swung her up the ladder.

George's feet clanged behind her on the steel, and she heard the sharp, laboring hiss of the breath of the man carrying her.

They were at the port. They entered, and the starman

dropped her roughly to the floor, and George clanged the door.

"You attended to the other ships?" George asked in the alien tongue of 'Brionimar.

"Yes," the starman said. "They will both explode shortly after takeoff."

"The others are all aboard? We are the only ones on this one?"

"Yes."

"Good. I will remember this. You have done a good day's work. You follow instructions well. I won't forget."

"Thank you."

"Watch the girl. I'll give the signal to leave."

"What do we do with her?"

"Dump her out as soon as we hit open space."

George's feet went forward. It was over, he was done. The issue lay between Bud and himself and between Bud and Herb, an exciting and dangerous situation that held, in its solution, the Oligarch's (and the Oligarchy's) fate: the fate of two worlds. The stakes were high. The Oligarch, thinking how free he was of the final responsibility, went first to wash the Earth germs from his contaminated hands.

Norma had not understood the conversation that muttered above her. But her terror was replaced by a sense of desperation. She moaned and opened her eyes.

The starman, looking down at her with a cold, impersonal gaze, grunted something unintelligible.

Norma struggled to her feet. He made no move to prevent or assist her. She steadied herself against the wall. Near her hand, in a clip holder, was a short, steel fire extinguishing rod. When the starman drew back his hand to hit her, she cringed away. Instinctively she found the rod and jerked it loose. Before she was aware of the action with her conscious mind, the starman sank to the floor, and the bar clattered from her nerveless fingers.

Heart racing she turned for the door. A moment later, she was outside, clambering down the ladder.

There were no taxis in sight. A jeep, driven by a uniformed messenger, drew to the curb. Herb, holding his breath, crossed to it. The driver cut the motor and got out.

When he disappeared in the building across the street, Herb slipped behind the wheel. He was a technician. He began to experiment. Recently acquired knowledge came to his aid.

After what seemed a timeless heat and an endless exposure, he had the motor running.

The C.I.A. man, who had come over on the subway from the House, stepped out into the sunshine. He surveyed the street with a practiced eye.

Herb spun the jeep away from the curb and sent it careening erratically toward the airport. The C.I.A. man (fairly confident of his identification of Herb) fired twice. Herb heard one of the bullets make an explosive pop as it passed near his ear. He hunched over the wheel and gunned the motor.

Norma stumbled from the ladder and started to run. The spider ships loomed menacingly behind her. An army guard started forward to question her, and a jeep leaped suddenly into sight from around the corner of the Administration Building. A heart beat later the jeep skewed around beside her, and Herb, his face twisted with hate and fury cried, "Where's Bud?"

One of the spider ships behind them became airborne; and then a second leaped away.

12

GEORGE was at the controls of the ship. As his hand hovered at the firing stud, he heard someone enter behind him. He turned.

It was the starman. His hair was matted with blood. There was a wild, rebellious glint in his eyes. He snarled like an animal.

"She hit me!" he cried. And then he smashed a fist into George's face. George went down and the starman stepped across him to the control panel. His resentment had been accumulating for a life time. He had just sabotaged two ships and sent his fellow starmen to death at the orders of the Oligarch; and he must have known (even if he told himself otherwise) that he, too, would not return to Brionimar: that alone of all who had been on the surface of Earth, the Oligarch would survive. But even in this knowledge, he had still remained loyal, caught like Herb, like his whole civilization, by the specter of chaos and held helpless. But now, thinking the destruction of Earth a certainty, his resentment rechanneled, he was able to strike—even kill, if necessary—the Oligarch in order to revenge himself upon the Earth girl who had struck him.

He snapped on the scanner and searched the airport. He saw Norma climb into the jeep. He sent the spider ship lumbering toward her. The jeep began to run.

The spider legs moved faster, and the ship, like a drunk, lurched awkwardly across the runway in pursuit. He was no pilot, but his hands jerked levers and twisted wheels and the ship moved. He sighted the underbelly heat ray.

Just as he depressed the firing lever, the ship stumbled across a transport plane that lay passively interdicting its path. The ship veered sharply to the left, throwing the sighting off target and causing the ray to turn the ground molten short of the speeding car.

The starman struggled to right his vehicle.

George found his weapon. He was numb and horrified. *If Norma were actually killed . . . if Bud found out . . . !*

George moved his weapon slowly so as not to attract the starman's attention. He was terribly, desperately frightened and unsure of himself.

The starman reached again for the firing lever. George shot twice. The starman's hand fluttered as if in indecision, and George shot again. The starman fell backwards, and the ship suddered to a stop.

George rolled to his feet. If Norma were not already dead, he must recapture her.

The C.I.A. man arrived in time to see the fantastic sight of a red and silver, tri-legged Leviathan from space stumbling after a surplus jeep. He slammed his car to a halt before the army guard station and cried, "Shoot him! Shoot him!" Demonstrating, he fired wildly in the direction of the jeep. "C.I.A.!" he cried. "Shoot, damn it!"

Herb heard the sinister pop of the hand gun and, glancing out of the corner of his eye, saw the rifles aligning themselves in his direction. He huddled lower over the wheel and screamed to Norma, "Hold on!"

Norma was transfixed with terror. The huge spider ship seemed almost upon them.

Herb was going too fast for the quick turn he attempted. The steering wheel was wrenched from his hand, and the jeep, like a tripped animal, twisted and threw itself to the ground and rolled over.

At the first bone shattering crash, Norma slammed into Herb, and his head cracked the steering wheel solidly.

Far to the west, the sky flashed dull red as the first spider ship exploded in flight. The sky flashed red again. Soldiers were running toward the wreck when the first shock wave rolled in.

In giant strides, George brought his own ship to the overturned jeep. It straddled the wreck like a defiant parent and seemed to challenge the advancing soldiers. George hurried to the port.

He slammed the door back and cried, "Don't shoot! Don't shoot!" The outer ladder fell away at the touch of his hand, and a second later his feet were hurrying down it.

Once on the ground, he was at the jeep in a heart beat. There was no blood, but both figures were very still. "Help me!" he cried to the arriving soldiers.

Two came forward, laid aside their guns, and together, with gentle hands, lifted Norma and then Herb free of the wreckage.

When they were stretched out on the ground, George knelt. Perspiration wetted his upper lip. He poised above Norma, seeking some sign of life, and he was aware of Herb stirring uneasily to his rear. Norma's eyelids fluttered, and a wave of relief and exultation enveloped George.

"She's all right," George said loudly. "Make sure the newspapers carry that. The girl is all right."

"Who is she?"

"She's one of ours," the Oligarch said with nice pos-

sessiveness. Bud would know better: that was all that mattered. He would know that the girl was Norma and that
the girl was safe. The delicate equation of his decision was
once more in balance. "Help me get them aboard the ship."

A small crowd was gathering, and an Army major pushed
his way forward. The C.I.A. man, overawed by the Oligarch's presence, and uncertain of what to do now, held
back watching.

"What's this?" the major demanded. "What's this?"

George stood up. "It's our personal problem. This renegade—"

"Is he the one who escaped from you? The nutty one?"

"Yes," George said.

"What about your other two ships? They exploded. They
just exploded."

Instantly the surrounding Earthmen rustled suspiciously.

"He—" George said . . . "It was sabotage. He is responsible. Terrible. Terrible. I'm stunned. We haven't any
time to waste. I've got to get this girl back to our big ship
out there in space for medical attention."

"We've sent for a doctor," the major said stiffly.

"We have doctors. For God's sake, man, help me get
them aboard. There's no time to stand here talking. We
have advanced techniques, if I can only get there in time,
that may mean the difference between life and death . . ."

The major hesitated. "All right. You two soldiers—
take the girl up the ladder."

"Herb, too," the Oligarch said. "If he survives, he will
be tried."

The major grunted at two more soldiers.

George followed them up the ladder. He greeted the
capture of Herb with bitterness. The game was over; he
had been denied the excitement of it being played out. And
yet there was relief: although he had once more been
thrust into a role of player, it was not of his own volition.
The conspiracy of events had released him from free choice.
It was not his fault that it was necessary to remove Herb
prematurely from the arena. He was uncomfortably aware
that the major was following him.

Inside the ship, George directed the soldiers to put their
burdens in the first compartment to the left. Then he turned

to the major. "Your prompt action may well have saved her life." He was tense and frightened. Now that he was sure it would be reported that a girl had been returned to the ship and hurried to medical attention, it was of paramount importance to get the soldiers and the major out of the ship. If Norma were unexpectedly to recover and begin to talk, the major might prove difficult to handle.

The crush of danger hung upon him. An instant, in which he wished to surrender and confess, was transplanted by dedication to victory. The sense of mission returned.

"I don't think I should permit you to leave, sir," the major said politely. "I've thought it over."

"Sir?"

"In view of what happened to the other two ships. How do you know this one hasn't been sabotaged, too? In your understandable anxiousness to get this girl . . ."

"I'm sure," George said evenly. "I tell you this ship is all right."

"Well, how do you know? Obviously, you knew the other two ships were all right, too; only they weren't . . ."

The Oligarch restrained an impulse to command. "This is too important a matter to delay with explanations."

The four soldiers clustering around the major seemed ominous.

"Our doctor will be here in a moment. Immediate aid can be given the girl."

George's hands trembled with rage and maddening anxiety. "I am going to takeoff immediately. Explanations can come later when the girl has been treated. I will hold you personally responsible for any further delay." He went toward the control room.

The major started to follow.

The Oligarch whirled to face him. "You will be responsible for her death. I am going to leave. If necessary, I will take all of you with me. You will have to use force to stop me."

The major stood with his hands clenched into fists at his sides. There was silence. The fists slowly unclenched.

"I would advise you to get off the ship at once," George said. He turned once more. This time he did not look back.

A thrill of uncertainty grew within the major. He

swallowed stiffly and then snapped angrily to the waiting soldiers, "All right, get the lead out! Let's go! Let's go, let's go!" He seemed to want to push them physically toward the exit.

The Oligarch was in the control room by the time they dropped off the ladder to the ground. A flick of the switch, and the ladder retreated. The ship trembled. A savage jab, and the ship became airborne. It was too late now for them to stop him. He had made a successful escape. He was weak with reaction. A few moments more . . .

He studied the dials. Earth fell away.

He could hurry. He only need save enough fuel for a tie in. He waited impatiently for altitude. Earth shrank. The features of her surface blurred. A cloud occluded her face completely. The air resistance lessened. Gravity weakened. He was able to pour the fuel into the space jets. He fired the first and second banks. Fuel gauges descended. Acceleration pressed against him like a hand. More jets. He was in a hurry. His mission was accomplished. Within two hours he would be out of the danger area of the Earth explosion. But he was not overly worried about that. He did not expect it until an hour or so after sunrise over Washington.

He locked the ship on automatic. Time enough later to finish computing the trajectory.

He was now free to dispose of Herb and Norma.

The sense of elation increased as he left the control room. He fingered his hand weapon and smiled to himself. Less than a minute later, he stepped into the doorway of the room containing the two people, his gun raised.

13

HERB HAD regained consciousness.

Herb shot, and flame leaped toward the Oligarch. The room roared with the explosion.

George jerked back, and in midmotion, something caught him low in his chest, on the left side of his body and slapped him savagely off his feet.

Incredibly, he had been hit!

He shook his head and got one knee under him. His left side was numb. He looked down and saw blood start to color his shirt.

He got to his feet and backed along the corridor. His knees were weak. He covered the door with a trembling hand and prayed for Herb to show himself.

The ship was silent.

He had to sit down. He wanted to be sick.

Perhaps Herb had taken the other door out!

He whirled.

No movement.

He had to have a place to hide. He had to hide, and wait, and when Herb came searching for him—

He staggered back. His side began to throb dully.

The ship was very quiet.

"He's out there," Herb said, knowing that his words would carry over the hidden microphones. "I will manage to kill him before we reach the big ship."

Norma was breathing shallowly, not yet fully recovered from the wreck. "What about Earth?"

"It's too late."

"If we could—if we could destroy the . . . that ship . . . if we could ram it: prevent it from setting off the charge . . ."

"It's too late," Herb said doggedly. But even with the words, he felt the first hesitant flicker of hope. If he could take over this ship, and with it assault the great ship in space, there capture the remote-control mechanism by which the charge would be detonated then perhaps Earth could really be saved. First kill the Oligarch. Then . . .

Norma whimpered to herself.

"You stay here," he hissed, too softly, he hoped for the microphones to pick up his voice.

Her eyes widened in protest. "Don't go. He'll . . ."

"Shhhhhh," he silenced her. Bending, he whispered, "I'll find him first. You'll be all right."

He left her. At the doorway, he looked back. She seemed crumpled and lifeless and defeated.

The Oligarch was somewhere to his left. In the corridor, waiting? Herb could not know. There was only one way to find out. He stepped from the room, gun ready to fire.

The corridor was empty.

Where? In the control room? In the office? In the kitchen? The messhall?

Herb moved forward silently.

The Oligarch had backed across the messhall. One hand clutched at his left side. His breathing was too loud. Herb would surely hear it.

He stood in the far doorway that opened into the short corridor leading to his office and that extended beyond his office to open into the main corridor. Herb would have to cross before its open face should he come forward. From the doorway, the Oligarch also commanded a view of the main messhall entrance, should Herb stop to inspect that room first. By ducking either in or out, he could place a protecting wall between himself and his pursuer. The Oligarch knew that Herb would come. His left side was terrifying testimony that the lifetime of conditioning had been stripped away.

It would be so easy to dart to his own office; but the unprotected space between him and it was a barrier more solid than a rock cliff. If Herb should emerge as he was making the exposed crossing, he would be a perfect target. His movements were sluggish. He had to locate Herb in order to know in which direction safety lay. But to be safe in the office, with the door barricaded . . .

Herb saw the drops of blood drying slowly along the floor of the corridor.

The Oligarch had entered the messhall. Herb approached cautiously.

Standing just outside, not exposing himself, he could see a clot of blood beyond the main door. Probably the Oligarch had hesitated there, undecided—or resting.

He held the gun more tightly. His heart beat rapidly, and

his mouth was dry. But he was not afraid. There was an iciness far down inside of him.

He stepped across the threshold, and just as suddenly, leaped back.

He heard the stumble of the Oligarch's fleeing feet, heard the office door open and slam.

Herb waited, listening: a feint?

No. There was no sound.

Again he stepped into the messhall. It was empty.

"Herb!" Norma called. "Herb! Are you all right?" She was running down the corridor toward him.

"Get back!" Herb called, but she came on, and then she was beside him.

"He's in the office. I'm going after him. You stay here."

"No. Leave him there. Prop the door. Keep him in. Take the ship . . ."

"I'm going in after him," Herb said. "I've got to. It's more than him, more than killing or getting killed. I've got to."

"It's so senseless," she said. "If we could get control of the ship . . ."

He shook his head. "You stay here!"

He walked across the messhall. He stepped out into the narrow corridor.

"Get away!" the Oligarch cried frantically. His voice was no longer vigorous, and it sounded pathetic and child-like through the door.

Herb, going toward it, said, "I'm coming in!" He tried the door. Locked.

He fired twice at the lock. He stepped back and kicked. The door swung inward.

The Oligarch did not fire. Herb, pressed against the wall, could not see into the room.

"I'm coming in, damn you!"

"Don't" the Oligarch cried weakly. "Please, don't. Don't now!"

Herb heard a gun clatter to the floor.

"Don't" the Oligarch moaned. "I've thrown it away. I'm helpless."

Herb balanced on the balls of his feet. Then, taking a deep breath, he stepped into the doorway, his body framed beautifully between the two jambs. He held his gun at ready and then lowered it.

The Oligarch was slumped over his desk.

Herb heard Norma come up behind him.

"He's dying," she said.

Reaction set in, and Herb's knees almost collapsed. His body was trembling and drenched with perspiration.

The Oligarch coughed.

The Oligarch said something in his own language.

"What?" Herb asked.

"Make him tell us. How we can keep them from setting off the explosion!" Norma said.

The Oligarch wanted to talk, and he made a motion— a feeble one—to silence them both. The girl's pathetic conviction that the explosion could be prevented infuriated the Oligarch. There was nothing she could do. The cleverness with which he had executed his mission defied time and eternity.

"It won't be set off in the big ship," the Oligarch said. "I had intended to leave you at the site, Herb, to trigger it personally." He spoke English and was disappointed to see that his vision began to mist. He would have liked to watch the girl's face. "But your later dream forms made me deny you martyrdom. I think I might have done it any way, if you hadn't left. You have the idealism. You were the one I had counted on. And after you, of course, there was only Bud."

Norma choked weakly and her knees half gave way. The sound was satisfying to the Oligarch.

"I told Bud the explosion was planted," the Oligarch said. "Then I . . . I told him . . ." He coughed again. "I told him that I had mailed his brother's head along with his confession to . . . to . . . Then I gave him a telephone number. He phones long distance, gives the number. At the bomb site, the receiver . . . lifts automatically . . . He says, 'Frank Council' . . . his brother's name . . . the key . . . The trigger falls." The Oligarch's hands scrabbled on the desk. "Don't you think he'll do it, in the knowledge of his own personal destruction? . . . Oh, he will, yes . . . And this is the final . . ." Blood dribbled from the Oligarch's mouth. "I didn't mail his brother's

head . . . I lied to him. Don't you see what a beautiful
. . . what a satisfying lie that was?" He laughed, coughed
again, and slumped forward. And the chase ended.

And Herb, looking at death, grabbed Norma by the arm
and ran toward the control room.

. . . And back on Earth, Bud Council sat sick and
trembling, his eyes fastened on the telephone beside him . . .

14

HERB THOUGHT first of the bomb site. The chill desert night
would be fresh upon it. Overhead, the pale moon would
ride toward the terrible Apocalypse of dawn—if Bud waited until then to make his phone call.

In a few hours (he thought) he could bring the spider
ship down upon the desert. The long dark night beyond
would give him time . . .

He visualized the scene as he remembered it from TV:
the single sentry shack where an Army guard protected the
alien handiwork.

"I'll talk to them when we land. I'll explain about Bud.
They'll find him and keep him away from the telephone.
They'll tell long distance operators not to place any calls
until they can find him. All I need is a few hours to convince someone that Bud, that Bud . . ."

Norma was in his arms, shaking hysterically. "He . . .
he did that to *Frank*. Bud did that!"

"We've got to hurry," Herb said.

She shivered against him. Gently he disengaged himself.

"In an hour, now . . ." he said. His hand rested on the
forward firing stud.

Rested and withdrew

"What's wrong?" Norma asked.

"The fuel. I haven't got enough left to brake the ship, to
turn it, and then land against Earth gravity."

"No," Norma said. "No! That can't be right!"

Herb re-sorted the information available from the dials, seeking a method to defy the dictates of inertia. Once more he weighed the remaining fuel against that necessary to brake and turn the ship, and still there was none left over to counteract Earth's gravity and the long planetfall. He projected trajectories.

"Maybe I can throw the ship in a long orbit," he said. "If I can kill the speed against the atmosphere . . ."

"Can you do it?"

Herb's hands eased fuel into the forward port jet and sparked it. "I'm tilting for the orbit."

The gauge dropped alarmingly, and as momentum changed, the center of gravity shifted. The ship nosed up and fell sideways and slipped away to the right.

Norma held her breath, afraid to interrupt even with encouragement.

"It's an ellipse," Herb said. "It's a long fall now, but I'm afraid to make it shorter." He set the controls.

"How long will it take?" Norma asked.

"I'll have to make half a dozen bounces. The first one won't be for nearly six hours . . . we won't be able to land until sunup."

Norma bit her lip. "But that's . . ."

"We won't have much time. We'll have to try to get to Bud ourselves."

When the time came, he turned to her. "I've got to hit the atmosphere now. We'll have to strap down."

Numb with tension, she sat in one of the shock-chairs and buckled herself in. Then, in his chair before the panel, Herb adjusted the buckles and waited the few remaining minutes. "This will be the worst," he said.

The ship hit the upper gases—gases, made by speed into an iron curtain; and as the air clawed at the strange shape of the ship, and as the interior cooling system whined into overdrive, he fought against wild, erratic movements, firing precious fuel to brake and stabilize . . . And then they were free, and shooting away along a shortened and slower ellipse.

Finally they were well into the atmosphere, but they were very high, too high to be more than a speck, so high that the sound spread too thinly to be heard on the surface.

"I'll set down outside Washington," Herb said. "Somewhere outside, where we can get away from the ship before they get there to start asking questions."

He released his blast, and the ship turned nose up. Gravity became heavier. The ship plummeted down.

"Here's the last of the jets," Herb hissed, and he eased them in, slowing the fall, slowing it . . .

Down the ship came.

The Earth expanded and a fantastically fast painter seemed to be sketching in the details of the landscape.

The sun was cut off by the horizon. A few lights sparkled in slowly waking Washington.

The jets sputtered, and the ship slipped; the jets caught, sputtered, and died.

Herb slammed on the low lift controls. The aerodynamically designed platform-like wings spun and hissed against the air. For a long moment, Herb was afraid they would not brake the fall, but the lifts caught, and the ship jerked, and Herb felt the bouyancy through the ship and through his mind and through his body.

15

LESS THAN five minutes later, they were stationary. The slowing lifts purred and the landing ladder hissed down.

Herb and Norma were upon it.

"About a—five hundred yards," Herb said. "Over that way: the highway. Let's go!"

Running at his side, Norma prayed desperately for a car to come soon.

They sprinted the last short distance because of growing headlights from the south. The car was coming fast, and Herb jumped into the roadway, waving his hands.

The car came on, sounding its horn hysterically. Herb waved and brakes squealed, and the car, at almost the last instant, veered away from him. The wind of its passing rustled his hair, and the horn still bleating, it slowly dwindled as the red tail lights faded into the darkness.

They waited. Five minutes passed.

"One's got to come!"

Early fire hung over the ocean from the as yet invisible sun. Dew lay on the plowed field behind them. The air was chill.

It seemed that the sun was symbolic fire slowly creeping and coloring the sky, slowly spreading over the world.

"What time is it?" Herb asked.

"Here's a car! Here's a car!"

Both of them leaped into the highway, waving and jumping up and down.

A long way away, the driver set his brakes, and the car coasted slowly, passed them and finally stopped.

They ran to it. Herb jerked open the door. "You've got to take us to Washington!" Herb said.

Norma, arriving behind him, said, "It's a matter of life and death!"

"Then get in," the man said.

Overhead a jet thundered in to locate the spider ship.

They were in the car.

"You've got to drive us to an apartment in Georgetown," Norma said.

"Lady, I've been driving all night."

"You've got to!" The urgency in her voice was nearly that of hysteria.

The driver started the car. "If it's that urgent . . ."

"It is," Herb said.

"Hurry, please, please hurry. Don't ask us to explain. Just hurry."

The driver stepped down on the gas. The car leaped ahead.

16

THE NEW buildings pressed against the new sidewalks. The streets were empty except for their car and a turret-like Mobile Sweeper whose gutter broom whispered against the curb. A light here and there in a window heralded the end of sleep. A lone car crossed at an intersection ahead, moving slowly as if fatigued by a night-long vigil.

The sun seemed reluctant to plunge the world into daylight; it balanced on the horizon in indecision. The moon was high and tiny and rode the growing blueness with a ghostlike pallor.

Herb, leaning forward tensely, thought: *Suppose Bud isn't there? Suppose he's somewhere else?*

"Turn left up here," Norma said. "It's only a few blocks."

The buildings anchored time to the Earth, encapsulating the past in steel and concrete. Morning shadows walked before the onrushing future.

"Here!" Norma cried.

The car braked to a stop.

The driver watched them run wildly, and an uneasiness settled upon him. He glanced to the east. The morning was chill. The excitement their urgency had generated had not vanished with their departure. What the devil? he thought. Whadda you suppose it's all about?

Inside, Norma said, "Third floor. He's got guards. I'll take the elevator. You take the stairs. I'll try to get the guards' attention."

Herb nodded. He bolted for the stairway. The carpet blanketed his footfalls. He heard the elevator doors click and the cage rattle upward.

First landing.

Silence.

Second landing.

His heart was loud. His feet became delicate, and he balanced on his toes, moving toward the final encounter.

There.

Norma had the guard. There was only one. She was speaking intently. The guard faced away from Herb.

Herb was in the corridor. He moved like a sigh, and the space between him and the guard shortened.

The guard turned, and Herb sprang. He crashed into the guard before the police automatic was clear of the shiny holster. The impact of his body spun the gun away.

They were down, wrestling viciously. Herb felt his head ring. He stiffled a cry. Pain nestled in his groin. He struck out.

The guard smashed an elbow into Herb's nose. He got up and kicked Herb in the face, and Herb jerked his leg savagely. Unbalanced, he went down. Herb was upon him. Breath hissed out, and Herb struck viciously with his gun butt. Panting, he stood.

"It's locked," he said, testing the door. Norma had recovered the guard's automatic. Whitefaced she stood.

Bloody nosed, bleeding, Herb threw himself into the panel. There was a great, kettle drum boom and the panel held. Again he slammed into it. It splintered away. He fought through the shards of maple, and was halfway into the room when Bud, looking up from the telephone, fired. Herb sighed and fell to the left and his gun slipped from his hand.

17

Bud, drained of color, cried "Hurry that call, operator!"

His gun was on the door when Norma filled it. "Stop, Bud!"

His eyes dulled. Conflicting emotions ran jagged edges over his face. One hand held the phone, the other the gun.

Norma was afraid to fire for fear she would miss. "I'll kill you if you try to stop me!" he screamed. He could not place the person in the doorway. And then he realized that it was the Devil cleverly disguised as his sister.

Norma stepped into the room, drawing closer. Her hand trembled violently. Bud was perspiring.

"Bud," she said. Her voice choked. "He didn't mail . . . he didn't mail the . . . package . . . the . . . the package." Tears ran down her cheeks.

"Get away! *Get away!*"

"He didn't mail it! No one need . . . you're safe . . . your secret . . . Put down the phone, Bud. Please, now. *Put down the phone!*"

Very clever nonsense, Bud thought, not believing it for a moment. What package? There was no . . . He must shoot this creature, now, before she . . .

The operator said in his ear: "Here is your number, sir."

"Put me on!"

The Devil was nearer. It was too late, he thought. Norma thought: Now, now, *now.*

Bud's hand whitened at the knuckles. His throat was dry. He was ready to scream the Name. He did not see Herb's hand close on the weapon nor see the muzzle elevate.

"Bud, Bud, Bud, please, please, Bud!" Norma said. The trigger of her gun would not respond.

"Get away," Bud said. He opened his mouth. "Frank C—"

And Herb fired until the weapon was empty.

There was echoing silence, and then Bud fell.

Norma was upon the telephone, ripping it free from the wall.

Herb staggered erect. Blood covered his suit. It hurt to move. A broken collar bone, he thought. Too high for the lungs.

He found Norma weeping hysterically in his arm. The other arm hung limp, and he winced with pain as he drew her tight.

He choked and bent to her ear and said, "Yes, yes," and suddenly he bent to kiss her tear stained lips, and he wanted to brush away the hair from her face, but that arm refused to move. She trembled against him, and he whispered, "Yes."

The sunlight came in the broad windows and slanted across Bud's face, boyish and petulant still in death; the sun, moving toward noon, bathed the whole awakening world with light, and far beyond it, in space but not in time, lay other stars.

And Herb felt free. For the first time in his life. Here, on Earth . . .

It was a wonderful feeling.

THE END

www.ingramcontent.com/pod-product-compliance
Lightning Source LLC
Chambersburg PA
CBHW020642180626
46816CB00003B/1093